"I ___
I have Petey to think about."

"I like Pete. A lot."

"I know, but Petey's full-time. He's number one. I can't date a man who doesn't understand…."

Ben reached out and took Maggie's hand in his. She clamped her lips shut, and he traced his thumb along the top of her hand. "I wouldn't have asked you out if I didn't understand you're a two-person package."

She lowered her gaze. "Oh."

With his hand, he lifted her chin until their gazes met. "That's not to say that I wouldn't also like to spend time with just you."

Maggie bit her bottom lip. "I'd like that, too."

"You wanna try this again?"

She nodded, and Ben leaned down and kissed the top of her head. He was glad she was willing, because he had a feeling she already owned his heart.

Books by Jennifer Johnson

Love Inspired Heartsong Presents

A Heart Healed
A Family Reunited
A Love Discovered

JENNIFER JOHNSON

and her unbelievably supportive husband, Albert, are happily married and raising three daughters: Brooke, Hayley and Allie. Besides being a middle-school teacher, Jennifer loves to read, write and chauffeur her girls. She is a member of American Christian Fiction Writers. Blessed beyond measure, Jennifer hopes to always think like a child—bigger than imaginable and with complete faith.

JENNIFER JOHNSON

A Love Discovered

HEARTSONG
PRESENTS

LOVE INSPIRED BOOKS

ISBN-13: 978-0-373-48702-8

A LOVE DISCOVERED

Printed in U.S.A.

Yes, my soul, find rest in God;
my hope comes from him.
—*Psalms* 62:5

This book is dedicated to my stepdad, a guy who's been in my life since I was three. He reads all my books, even though he is a sci-fi fan who wants to hurl when he gets to the mushy parts. Dad, it's not Captain Kirk falling in love with Dr. Spock's sister all while saving the world from a Klingon invasion, but it is dedicated to you! Try to hold back the vomit! Love ya!

Chapter 1

Pain shot through Ben Jacobs's cheek. He sat up in bed and cupped his hand around the wound. After blinking several times to orient himself, his gaze locked on a brown-haired toddler holding a small red fire truck. His nephew squealed with delight then raced out of the room as fast as his chubby legs and feet would allow.

Releasing a groan, Ben flopped back in bed and rubbed the spot Ronald had clobbered. *He just had to hit the bone, didn't he?*

He glanced at the alarm clock on the bedside table then hopped up again. It couldn't possibly be seven o'clock. He'd set the alarm last night. He remembered doing it. Growling, he grabbed a worn pair of jeans and an old work shirt out of the closet and threw them on.

Without a doubt, his older brother, Kirk, had already fed the animals and checked on the apple and peach trees. Had probably even taken a look at the pumpkin patch.

October was a busy month for the Jacobs Family Farm in Bloom Hollow, Tennessee. Schools brought their students on field trips to enjoy the activity center and petting zoo and to pick apples and pumpkins. His parents' bed-and-breakfast, gift shop and small café had been extra busy this season, as well.

He pulled the comforter up over the pillows at the top of the bed. Knowing the bed wasn't made well enough for his sister-in-law's liking, he shut the bedroom door, all the while expecting a good tongue-lashing from her later that night. Biting back bitterness, he made his way to the bathroom to wash his face and brush his teeth.

It wasn't Callie's business if he made his bed or not. He was a grown man. Besides, he and his brother had lived together in this house for several years before Kirk and Callie got married. Ben hadn't planned to return to Bloom Hollow and his family's farm, but he hadn't had a choice. And he hated being stuck here.

Finished getting ready for the day, he walked past his twin nephews' room. His old bedroom. Though he loved the boys, it still felt like a knife twisting his gut every time he saw his old room painted a pale green and covered in elephants, lions, giraffes and other jungle animals. The living room was worse. Ruffled curtains. Flower-covered throw pillows. And Callie had some weird fetish for teddy bears. A guy couldn't sit anywhere without some furry critter with a tag hanging from its neck staring at him.

"What time is she supposed to get there?"

Callie's voice drifted down the hall. Ben nodded to her as he walked into the kitchen, opened the cabinet and grabbed a granola bar. He gulped down a quick glass of milk. He'd eat the bar on the way to the barn.

She continued her phone conversation. "Don't worry. I'll come over and make sure everything looks nice."

Ben opened the back door. Callie grabbed his arm then lifted her pointer finger for him to wait a minute. He glanced at the kitchen clock. Fifteen minutes had already passed, and he was anxious to help his brother and Dad. Especially since he and Dad weren't on the best of terms.

"Okay. I'll see you in a few minutes, Jane. Bye now."

She shoved the cell phone into her front jeans pocket and turned to Ben. She wrinkled her nose and lifted her shoulders. "I need a favor, Benny."

Even at twenty-four and as a college graduate, whenever Callie called him by the name she'd given him when he was just a kid, he couldn't help but smile. "What?"

"I need you to watch the boys."

"What? Why?"

"Jane Williams, you know the elderly lady I kind of watch out for? Well, her great-niece is moving in with her today, and Jane's blood pressure has been high, so she hasn't been able to clean the house much, so she asked me to help…."

Ben lifted his hand. He really didn't care about the details of some lady in town. "Where's Mom?"

"She already left for a doctor's appointment. He wants to check her sugar levels again."

"What about Pamela?"

"On her way to school."

Ben bit back a growl. "Callie, I can't. I gotta help Kirk and Dad."

Callie shook her head. "I called Kirk before I talked with Jane. They're fine. They've finished most of the chores, and…"

And his dad probably thought he was the biggest mess-up on the planet. Kirk had always been the epitome of a perfect son, working hard on the farm, saving money and going to church. His sister, Pamela, had had a hard time when her husband left her with two small children and she had to move in with their parents. But she'd always worked hard, saved money and gone to church. Now she was back with the girls' dad and about to graduate college with an accounting degree.

Then there was Ben. Mike and Tammie Jacobs's baby. His parents' church friends' warnings echoed through his mind. "Quite a pistol, ain't he?" and "Mark my words. That one'll give you grief."

"So, will you watch them?"

Ben blinked away his thoughts and focused on Callie. She stuck out her bottom lip. "Please."

"Sounds like I don't have a choice."

Callie stood on tiptoes and kissed his cheek. "Thanks. I owe you one." She grabbed her purse off the counter. "I'll be back for lunch."

Ben gasped. "What? That's like four hours from now."

"Don't worry. I'll stop and get some fast food."

Before he could respond, Callie rushed out the back door. Ben turned and looked at his nephews, who stood in front of the television clapping their hands and swaying to some song on a cartoon program.

Half a year ago, he'd have never dreamed babysitting toddlers would have been in his future. He'd hoped to be with a big company in a city somewhere putting his electrical engineering degree to work. Instead, he'd spend the next few hours singing songs, changing diapers and filling sippy cups. Proof that God really did have it in for him.

"I think God has it in for me." Maggie Grant blew out a long breath as she accepted a welcoming hug from her great-aunt, Jane Williams.

"Nonsense." Aunt Jane released Maggie then adjusted

the floppy straw hat she always wore. It had been summer the last time Maggie had seen her aunt and the hat had sported a long, yellow, flowered ribbon in honor of the season. This time a bright orange ribbon covered in black cats wrapped around it in celebration of the month of October.

"Where's that great-great-nephew of mine?" Aunt Jane smacked her lips together, and Maggie noted the bright pink shade painted on them. The same shade she had worn for as long as Maggie could remember.

Maggie cringed as she opened the back door of the midsize car that had seen many better days. After hours of crying, talking, vomiting and then more of all three, her carsick three-year-old son had finally fallen asleep a few miles outside Bloom Hollow. She hated the idea of waking him up. "He just fell asleep, Aunt Jane."

"Well, we can't leave him out here."

"I know."

"Carry him in the house. We'll put him in my bed."

Maggie shifted her weight from one foot to the other. If only it were that easy. Petey gave her fits when he didn't get his full nap. She'd prefer to just camp outside in the car until the little guy woke up on his own.

Aunt Jane motioned to the house. "Come on, now. We don't want to stay out in this wind all day."

Maggie inhaled the slight breeze that kissed her face and gently feathered her hair. The temperature was ideal. Nonetheless, Aunt Jane wrapped her sweater tighter around her waist. Maggie couldn't argue with the woman. All she could do was pray Petey would stay asleep. If she was careful, maybe she could slip him out of the car seat, walk gently into the house and lower the two of them into her aunt's rocking chair.

"Maggie, dear, what's that in his hair?"

Petey whimpered and shifted in Maggie's arms as Aunt Jane scratched at a brown spot on his temple.

Maggie furrowed her brow. "I think it's vomit."

The older woman scrunched up her nose. "Oh."

"I told you God hates me. We spent ten hours in the car. Petey puked four times, I had to change a flat tire and I almost ran out of gas because I forgot to check the gauge before we hit the seventy-seven-mile stretch with no gas stations."

"You made it." Aunt Jane opened the front door of the house. "If you ask me, that shows He's looking out for you."

Maggie allowed her aunt's positive attitude to lift her spirits. She could use some rose-tinted glasses. Maggie had spent all of Petey's life wallowing in self-pity. Her young son deserved more than that. His father would have wanted more for him.

The loneliness and pain she'd pushed to the deepest recesses of her heart bubbled up, and Maggie swallowed the knot in her throat. Paul had died serving their country in Afghanistan when Maggie was seven months pregnant with Petey. He'd never had the chance to hold his son, and she'd never had the chance to say goodbye to the man she loved so desperately.

Shaking the thought away, Maggie followed Aunt Jane into the house. The scent of apple cider wafted through the air, and Maggie's stomach growled. Realizing it had been hours since she'd eaten, she hoped her great-aunt had something she could eat once Petey woke up.

Aunt Jane motioned down the hall. "Come on. Let's lay him down."

Maggie shook her head. "It's okay. I'll just sit in the rocking chair until he wakes up."

Her aunt clicked her tongue. "Nonsense. You're hungry. I heard your stomach rumbling."

Maggie's cheeks warmed. "He'll wake up."

"No, he won't. You'll see."

Frustrated, Maggie bit her tongue and followed her aunt down the hall. Aunt Jane folded the covers back then Maggie bent down and laid him on the bed. *Please, God, don't let him wake up.* Petey sat straight up, opened his eyes and stuck out a quivering bottom lip. Maggie reached for him, but Aunt Jane stopped her. The elderly woman patted his back.

"Lie down now, Pete. Your nap isn't over."

Her tone left no room for arguing and to Maggie's surprise Petey flopped back onto the bed and closed his eyes. Aunt Jane pressed her finger against her lips and nodded toward the door.

Once in the hall, Maggie stammered, "I can't believe he lay back down."

"He's tired. Why wouldn't he?"

"Because he *never* does that."

"Hmm, you baby the boy too much." She reached up and squeezed Maggie's cheek. "Sounds like my niece might need me every bit as much as I need her."

Maggie bit her tongue again as she followed her aunt into the kitchen. She wouldn't mention the frying pan she'd spied on the nightstand beside Aunt Jane's bed. Before she'd decided to move in with her aging relative, Maggie's mom had warned her that Aunt Jane was putting things away in odd places.

Maggie's stomach growled again when she spied the platter of fried chicken and bowls of mashed potatoes and green beans on the counter. "Aunt Jane, you shouldn't have."

"I didn't cook all this." She lifted up swollen, wrinkled

hands. "It's been quite some time since these hands have let me cook a feast like that."

"Then where—"

"My friend Tammie Jacobs cooked it. She owns a farm a few miles out, and her daughter-in-law, Callie, takes care of me most days." Aunt Jane laughed. "When she ain't chasing after those wild twin boys of hers."

Maggie opened the cabinet and pulled out two plates. Memories of the women from her grandmother's small country church getting together to cook dinners for shut-in seniors washed over her. It had been a long time since she'd been part of a church family who looked out for one another. She hadn't forgotten about God. Of course, she still believed in Him, but she'd been busy caring for Petey and working at a local supermarket.

The doorbell rang, and Maggie jumped and pressed her palm against her chest. *Please, Lord, don't let Petey wake up.*

Aunt Jane clicked her tongue. "I bet that's Tammie's boy Ben. She called and said she'd forgotten to send the chocolate pie with our meal."

Maggie licked her lips. "Chocolate pie?"

Aunt Jane nodded. "She asked about your favorite dessert. I tell you, that woman is a gem. Almost as sweet as me." She cackled as she pointed toward the door. "If you'll answer the door, I'll find the salt and pepper."

Maggie chose not to comment when her aunt opened one of the drawers in the refrigerator. She made her way to the front of the house and opened the door. A tall, dark-haired man with piercing, deep blue eyes smiled at her, and she found herself swallowing a knot in her throat. After blinking several times, she opened the door wider. "Come on inside. You must be Ben."

He bit his bottom lip, and Maggie felt in her own body

the blush that crept up his neck and cheeks. "And you must be Maggie."

He continued to stand there, and Maggie's heartbeat raced inside her chest. She motioned inside. "You can—"

Shaking his head, he handed her the pie. "I can't stay. Mom wanted me to drop this off to y'all." He tipped his head. "It was nice meeting you, Maggie."

She nodded in agreement then he hopped off the front porch. "Bye," she whispered, then straightened her shoulders to knock some sense back into her brain. She was simply exhausted. That was all.

Her aunt yelled from the kitchen. "I found the shakers. Was that Ben?"

"Yes," Maggie hollered back as she shut the door then peeked out the window to watch his truck drive down the road.

"Did he want to stay and eat with us?"

Maggie shook her head to clear her thoughts once more. She walked back into the kitchen and sighed at the sight of a warm, home-cooked meal. "No, he didn't."

"Well, all right, then. Let's say grace then get to eating." After prayer and filling her plate, Maggie stuck her finger in the mashed potatoes then licked it. Mmm, so good. Warmth filled her as she listened to her aunt chatter on about the people of Bloom Hollow. Moving to Tennessee might be just what she needed.

Chapter 2

A cool seventy degrees and a cloudless sky, Ben Jacobs breathed in the perfect day for fifty kindergarteners to visit the Jacobs Family Farm. The Smoky Mountains swathed the backdrop of the farm in beauty and majesty. Rows of apple and peach trees billowed in front of the mountains, while vines plump with ripened pumpkins adorned the ground near the activity center. Though he missed the conveniences of the city, he couldn't deny the beauty of his home.

Kirk, Callie and Pamela's husband, Jack, had chased after the five-year-olds at the petting zoo and the activity center most of the morning. Having settled the kids at picnic tables, Ben knew mere minutes would pass before the kindergarteners would finish with lunch and grow eager to race to the pumpkin patch to pick out a pumpkin to take home.

While Callie spoke with the teachers, Kirk and Jack

read a story to the students about growing a garden. Ben looked back at Pamela spinning their nephews, Ronald and Teddy, on the merry-go-round. Jealousy swelled within him. His brother and sister had everything. Spouses. Kids. Even the careers they wanted.

Maggie's face drifted to his mind. He couldn't recall the last time he'd been so drawn to a woman simply by her opening a front door. But there was something about that blond-haired, blue-eyed beauty that made her keep popping up in his thoughts at odd times of the day. He shook his head. What pretty woman would want to get messed up with a jobless guy with a ton of debt?

He blew out a sigh, contemplating his siblings again. Having idolized both of them growing up, he was happy for their contentment. His parents had said that they worried Kirk and Pamela felt cheated because there was only a year between them, which meant neither of them got a lot of individual attention. Ben had come along four years after Pamela and was blessed with never-ending doting by his parents. And yet what he wanted was the closeness he saw in his brother and sister.

His cell phone rang. Taking it out of his front pocket, he spied his college best friend's nickname on the screen. He pressed the button and placed the phone against his ear. "Hey, Taylor, what's up?"

"Got a game going tonight. You in?"

He gripped the phone tighter and shoved his free hand into his front jeans pocket. His heartbeat raced with the need to say yes. "What time?"

"Ten. Come on, man. It's been forever since you played."

Swallowing the knot in his throat, he pulled his hand out of his pocket and raked his fingers through his hair.

He had to say no. Why was it so hard to spit out the two-letter word?

"Rick's gonna be there. You know what a loser he is."

Rick Mason. What a total goof. The man played poker every time Taylor asked. Never won a game. Even lost the shoes on his feet one night. Ben hadn't heard anything about Rick in over a year. "I thought he graduated and moved away somewhere."

"No, man. He dropped out. Works at the gas station on the corner of Bell Street and Main."

"Why'd he drop out?"

"Couldn't pay tuition, I guess. How would I know? Are you in or out?"

The kindergarteners stood and dumped their sacks in the garbage cans. Some were already running toward the pumpkin patch a few yards away. He needed to get off the phone and help the teachers and his family. He sucked in a deep breath, willing his mouth to say what his mind knew he should. "I can't. Sorry, man."

Not waiting for Taylor to try to change his mind, Ben hung up, turned off the phone and shoved it into his pocket. He strode toward the pumpkin patch, determined to will his thoughts to wrap around five-year-olds seeking the carve-worthy fruit.

"Ben!"

He glanced behind him and saw his mother waving him over to her. She held Ronald on her hip and gripped a not-too-happy Teddy's hand.

Walking toward her, he noticed her hands shaking. He grabbed Ronald out of her arms. "Mom. You're shaking something fierce."

She nodded. "I know. I've waited too long to eat. My sugar's dropped. The boys need to be laid down for their nap. Will you take them so I can get a bite to eat?"

"Of course." He bent down and lifted up Teddy with his free arm. "I'll walk you to the house."

She lifted her hand. "No. I'll be fine. Take them to their cribs."

"Mom."

"I promise. I'm fine."

He watched her walk toward the farm's main house, which his parents also used as a bed-and-breakfast. Ronald laid his head on Ben's shoulder, while Teddy squirmed to get out of his grasp. He looked down at his nephew and lifted his brow. "You're not going anywhere, little man."

Teddy frowned and continued to struggle against Ben's hold. Once his mother stepped into the house, he put the boys down and texted Kirk to tell him what had happened. Kirk texted right back that they could handle the guests.

Feeling more like the go-to errand boy than an educated engineer, Ben picked up the boys and carried them back to Kirk and Callie's. Once inside, he washed the bulk of dirt off the boys' faces and hands, changed their diapers then put them in their cribs. Ronald was asleep before Ben laid him down. Not Teddy. He fought and whined a few minutes before grasping his tattered blue blanket and snuggling it against his cheek.

Ben shut the door to their bedroom and released a sigh. He wanted to pull his phone out of his pocket, call Taylor and tell him to set up a place for him. But he couldn't. His student loans were astronomical because of his poker habit, and he'd promised his dad. The thought of hurting Mike Jacobs a second time caused pain to lace through Ben's veins.

He thought of Maggie again then pushed her out of his mind. The woman had some kind of wacko hold on him, and he definitely didn't need to worry about women right now.

The urge to play the card game wrapped itself around him like a boa constrictor squeezing the life out of its prey. If Ben hoped to stay true to his promise, he'd have to find something to do.

He walked out the back door. Spying a pile of wood that needed to be chopped, he grabbed an ax and finished off the chore. He noticed some ripe tomatoes in the garden, so he grabbed Callie's basket and collected tomatoes, peppers and green beans. Taking the produce inside, he washed all of them then snapped the beans. Wishing the boys would wake up, he peeked in their door. Both slept soundly.

Releasing a sigh, he walked back to the kitchen. He'd have to see what Callie had in the pantry and refrigerator because he was making dinner.

Maggie exhaled a long breath. Her aunt's finances were a complete mess. She'd taken a second mortgage on the house and hadn't made a payment in months. One late notice for the electric bill. Two late notices for the water. *I can't believe it hasn't already been turned off.*

She spied the property taxes for the house and consignment store. The large sum was due by the end of the year, in only two months. Since her aunt had already added Maggie's name to her personal bank account, Maggie checked her balance online. Her aunt had the funds to get the water bill caught up and for part of the electric bill, but not the mortgage.

Scrolling through her aunt's debits, she gasped at the various purchases for the consignment store. She realized the garbage pickup bill hadn't been paid, either, nor the phone bill.

Maggie bit her bottom lip as she looked up the balance on her own checking account. Though thankful for the military pension she received since Paul's death, it wouldn't be enough to cover her aunt's past due and current bills. Placing her elbows on the table, she leaned forward and rubbed her temples. *Think, Maggie. How should you handle this?*

She could call her mom. Anne Richmond owned a successful realty business. She and Maggie's sister, Darla, had superb business sense and had been able to continue to thrive despite the struggling economy. Maggie shook her head. She didn't want to call them. Mom wanted Aunt Jane to sell the family's home and consignment business and move in with her. But her mom lived on the other side of the state, near Jackson. No more Smoky Mountains. No more family business. Maggie knew Aunt Jane would never want to do that.

Sitting back in the chair, she straightened her shoulders and folded her hands together. She'd just have to go to the various businesses, talk with them and pay what she could. Her aunt had been part of this community since birth, and Maggie assumed the people of Bloom Hollow would be willing to work with her. At least, she hoped they would.

Glancing at the clock, she knew Petey would wake up any moment. Taking him with her would pose quite a challenge, but what choice did she have?

"Penny for your thoughts."

Maggie startled at the voice behind her and turned around. Aunt Jane giggled and placed her hand over her mouth. "Didn't mean to scare you, Maggie, dear."

Maggie smiled. "I know." She stood up and gave her aunt a morning hug. "How are you feeling this morning?"

"Right as rain, and my blood pressure is terrific."

"Did you check it?"

"No, but I can tell."

Maggie pursed her lips and shook her head as she took her aunt's arm. "Come on."

Her aunt clicked her tongue. "All these young girls thinking they can boss an old woman around."

Her aunt's tone was teasing, but Maggie wouldn't have minded if it wasn't. She didn't want anything to happen to her aunt, and Maggie would stay on her if she had to. Aunt Jane sat down at the kitchen table, and Maggie placed the blood pressure cuff on her arm. Once the machine finished, Maggie grinned. "You're right, Aunt Jane. Your blood pressure is great today."

"I told you." She giggled and shuffled her eyebrows. "Haven't watched a single Robert Redford film in days. No reason for my heart to be racing."

Maggie chuckled as she put the machine back in its container. "As soon as Petey wakes up, I'm going to head to town and pay a few bills."

Her aunt's face flushed and she ducked her head. "I've never been very good about paying bills, even when I was younger."

Maggie scrunched her nose. "You're a bit behind."

"I know." She straightened in her chair. "Why don't you head on into town and let Petey stay with me? I'll get his breakfast, and we'll work on some reading and writing."

"Aunt Jane, he's three."

Her aunt shook her head. "Quit holding this little guy back. You're never too young to learn." She lifted her arm and pretended to make a muscle. "And I'm fit as a fiddle. I can take care of the boy."

Maggie chewed the inside of her mouth. In the week she'd been in Bloom Hollow, she had been surprised how well her aunt got around, even with her swollen hands. And Petey absolutely adored the elderly woman. He seemed to obey her every command, and yet challenge Maggie at each turn.

Aunt Jane patted Maggie's arm. "He'll be fine. You baby him too much."

Maggie bit back a retort. She'd grown tired of well-meaning family members and friends telling her she babied Petey. She'd make no apologies for wanting to enjoy every moment of her son's life. He was her living, breathing connection to Paul and probably the only child Maggie would ever have.

Aunt Jane rubbed her hands together. "If I can still care for five babies in the nursery during Sunday school, I can certainly care for one three-year-old boy."

Maggie chuckled. That had been another surprise she'd witnessed when they attended church a few days ago. She'd been stunned watching her aunt race from one infant to the other without a care in the world. The mothers seemed to adore Aunt Jane. Not that Maggie could blame them. And she couldn't deny being in church had been nice all the way around.

"Okay. You've convinced me." She lifted her brows. "But are you sure you *want* to be stuck with a three-year-old all morning?"

Aunt Jane pointed to her chest. "Pete has been a complete joy to this old woman's heart. He's probably the reason my blood pressure's so good." She nudged Maggie's elbow. "And like I said, I haven't had time to watch Robert Redford."

Maggie nodded as she grabbed her purse off the counter. "I'll be back before lunch."

Aunt Jane snapped her fingers. "Wait a minute." She picked up several dishes off the counter. "I forgot to take these to Tammie at church. Would you mind to run them by their farm? It's not hard to find."

Maggie listened as her aunt gave directions to the Jacobses' house. She remembered meeting Tammie at church. She'd been kind and anxious for Maggie to meet the rest of her family. Apparently, most of them hadn't been able to attend because they'd shared a stomach bug. Her heart fluttered when she thought of Tammie's son Ben. He hadn't been at church, either, and Maggie had been surprised at the disappointment that washed over her when she didn't get to see him again.

Waving goodbye to her aunt, Maggie headed out the door, praying the various companies would have compassion. She pondered the many times she'd uttered quick prayers since moving in with her aunt. She was enjoying a bit of fellowship with her heavenly Father again, and to her surprise, she looked forward to seeing Tammie again. Secretly, she hoped to see Ben, as well.

Chapter 3

Maggie drank in the sight of the Jacobs Family Farm. She drove closer to the white two-story house with a gray roof and dark green shutters. A yellow-and-orange wreath hung from the door welcoming all visitors. Matching the wreath, potted mums sat on the covered porch and lined the steps. An elaborately designed wooden sign read Jacobs Bed and Breakfast.

She turned off the engine, grabbed the dishes from the passenger seat and got out of the car. Beyond the house, she spied an activity center of sorts with an oversize slide and several hay bales piled on top of each other. She couldn't tell for sure, but it looked as if there was a petting zoo past that. She sucked in a breath at the most awe-inspiring sight around the property, the Smoky Mountains rising and falling in the distance. Having decided to move, she feared she'd miss the flat, open spaces of her Texas home, but already she'd lost her heart to the Tennessee Mountains.

Another building sat to the right of the house, sporting a café and gift shop sign. The building was white, like the house, but several pumpkins, potted mums and baskets of apples covered the ground in front. A giant-size wooden chair rested a little ways in front of the café and gift shop with the farm's name painted in dark green letters, a perfect setup for families and friends to climb up into it and take pictures.

Beyond the shop, she saw an additional farmhouse to the right. On the left, she noticed the edge of a log cabin behind the bed-and-breakfast, an orchard of apple and peach trees and even the corner of a large pumpkin patch. She bit the inside of her lip. *This place is amazing.*

"Hi, Maggie. How are you today?"

Maggie startled and gripped the dishes tighter. She'd met him only one time, but she recognized the voice immediately. She looked up at Ben standing on the front porch and wondered how long he'd been there as she took in the beauty of the place.

She cleared her throat then lifted the dishes higher. "I'm just returning the dishes to Tammie."

"You just missed her. She and Dad went to town half an hour ago."

Maggie nodded, wishing she sounded as unaffected by his presence as he did by hers. She tried to figure a way to keep her knees from feeling so wobbly all of a sudden. Ben had the same short, dark hair, but today dark stubble traced his strong jawline. Beneath full eyebrows, bright blue eyes seemed to bore into her. Broad shoulders filled the tan button-down shirt tucked into a pair of well-worn blue jeans. Brown cowboy boots completed a look that made her heartbeat race in a way she hadn't experienced in years.

A slow grin spread over his lips, exposing straight, white teeth. She blinked and swallowed the knot in her throat, trying to force her brain to think of something, anything, to say.

He motioned to the front door. "You wanna come in?"

Her mouth continued to refuse to work as she nodded and walked up the steps. High school. Senior year. That was the last time she'd been left speechless. It was the day the hunky quarterback Paul Grant had asked her on a date. They'd gotten married nine months later, right after graduation.

She followed Ben into the kitchen and set the dishes on the counter. Rubbing her hands together, she mentally shook her head. She wasn't some silly seventeen-year-old girl. Ten years had passed. She'd had a child and lost the love of her life. She wouldn't allow some ridiculous instant attraction to overtake her every thought and move, and she would vehemently deny that the image of him standing in her aunt's doorway had filled her mind on multiple occasions the past week.

"Our first meeting was a bit rushed since I had to make it to the bank before they closed." He extended his hand. "So let's start over. Ben Jacobs."

Maggie took his hand, ignoring its calloused strength and the tingling shooting through her hand and up her arm. "Maggie Grant."

"It's very nice to meet you, Maggie."

Was it her imagination, or did Ben linger on the word *very* a bit longer than necessary? Not that it mattered if he did. She most definitely had not moved to Bloom Hollow to find a man. She lifted her chin, determined to conquer her wayward mind. "Your mother made us a delicious welcome-to-town dinner."

"She's a good cook. That's for sure."

"The chocolate pie was delicious. It's my favorite."

Ben rubbed his stomach. "One of mine, too. You should try my sister's apple crisps sometime." He shook his head. "Dad tells her God's going to make that her job in heaven. To make apple crisps all day, every day."

She chuckled and rubbed her hands together again, contemplating her words. The flutters in her gut were making her light-headed. She needed to get out of there. *Maybe I'm just hungry. It is lunchtime, and I just spent the past several hours requesting extra time to pay off overdue bills. Anyone would feel anxious.*

A toddler raced into the room, grabbed Ben's pants and pointed to his own mouth. "Eat," he said.

Ben bent down and picked up the child. "Is Teddy hungry?"

The boy nodded, pointed to the refrigerator then back at his mouth. "Eat."

Maggie lifted her purse strap higher on her shoulder. She raised her hand to say goodbye when another toddler wrapped his arms around her leg. He giggled, and Ben scooped the second boy into his free arm.

"Eat!" screamed the first child. She believed Ben had called him Teddy.

Her heartbeat raced anew at the vision of the burly man holding two small boys in his arms. "Would you like some help?" she asked.

"Nah. Do it all the time."

He placed one boy and then the other on booster seats. Grabbing a box of cheese crackers out of the cabinet, he put a handful on the table in front of each boy.

"These are your sons?" she asked.

Ben guffawed. "No."

Surprised at his emphatic response, she stepped back.

He lifted his hand. "Not that I don't adore my nephews. I'm just not ready for fatherhood." Her heartbeat slowed as he opened the refrigerator and pulled out a container of what looked like leftover spaghetti. "They're my brother, Kirk, and sister-in-law, Callie's, boys."

"Oh, these are the twins Tammie told me about at church."

Ben shoved the dish in the microwave. "We were all fighting a bug over the weekend. Didn't make it to church. We'll be there this week, though."

Maggie nodded. Disappointment at his words about fatherhood weeded through her stomach. She really had to get out of there. She shouldn't have come in the house to begin with. Should have just given him the dishes and gotten back in the car. She lifted her hand. "Nice talking with you. I'm sure I'll see you at church."

She left the house and hopped into her car. She had no reason to feel the loneliness that seemed determined to wrap itself around her. The bill collectors had given her some time to come up with the money her aunt owed. She'd had a few hours to herself while her aunt cared for Petey. And yet, sadness pressed against her heart. She turned the key in the ignition. She just needed to go home.

"She ran out of here pretty quick, didn't she, boys?" Ben scooped spaghetti onto two plastic plates. Using the fork, he cut the noodles into tiny pieces. He taste-tested a bite. Satisfied the food wouldn't burn their mouths, he placed the plates on the table.

Teddy cackled as he shoved a large handful in his mouth, while Ronald picked up his spork and tried to shovel some on the utensil. Ben grinned. Eighteen months old, and the boys already had unique personalities.

He hated that he hadn't been able to find a job in Knoxville. He loved the city. Enjoyed the hustle and bustle, the convenience of stores on every corner, the ability to watch a movie or go to a restaurant without driving ten or more minutes.

Yet he couldn't deny the joy of getting to know his nephews better. Before he left for college, he had a strong relationship with Pamela and Jack's girls. Emma and Emmy were excited when he came home for visits, and they'd picked up their close relationship right where they'd left off. But the boys had been hesitant to warm up to their uncle Ben when he moved home right after their first birthday. The poker games had been intense his last year of school, and he hadn't visited the farm enough.

Guilt filled him as he poured milk into the boys' sippy cups. He owed more money to the government than he should. He'd lost his dad's trust. And he still fought the urge to call up Taylor and have him save him a spot at the poker table.

"Mo'!" yelled Teddy.

Ben placed the cups in front of the boys then picked up Teddy's empty plate. He bent down in front of his strong-willed nephew. "Say please."

Teddy cackled and nodded his head several times. "Pease."

Ben rustled his hair. "Good job, buddy."

The back door opened, and his mom walked inside. "We're back."

The boys shifted in their seats, trying to get to their grandmother. She touched both of their heads. "You boys keep eating. Gramma's not going anywhere."

"Where's Dad?"

"Went to the barn to check on something." His mother pointed to the dishes on the counter. "Did Jane's niece bring those by?"

Ben nodded, and she snapped her fingers. "I owe Jane some money for a couple of outfits I bought the boys at the consignment store. I was going to give her the check."

He shrugged. "I gotta go by the hardware store and pick up a fuse. The truck's brake light is out. You want me to drop it by?"

"Yes. That would be wonderful. Jane would never in a million years ask for the money, and I've had it in my purse a week."

"She probably forgot you owe her."

His mother laughed. "You're probably right."

She dug through her purse and handed him the check. He pointed to the boys. "You want me to wait until the destruction is finished?"

Ronald laughed then blew spaghetti out of his mouth. Teddy quickly mimicked his brother. Mom shooed Ben toward the back door. "I've got them. Run that check to Jane for me."

Ben walked to the truck and drove to Jane's house. He pulled onto her street and saw Jane and Maggie talking to their neighbor. Ben recognized the guy. Couldn't remember his name. He'd graduated with Pamela. But even from a distance he could tell the guy was flirting with Maggie.

Jealousy swelled in his chest. From what he remembered of the guy, he'd been a jerk. Even if Ben's recollection came from a middle-school perspective, Maggie could do better. He scrunched up his nose. What was he thinking? He'd met the woman two times, and he was worried about who she dated. *Get a grip, Jacobs.*

Jane waved as he pulled into the driveway. He noticed

Maggie bite her bottom lip and looked toward the house. Funny, she'd seemed friendly at first. He'd been attracted to her. After all, who wouldn't be? She was gorgeous. Long, straight blond hair. Blue eyes that made a guy feel like he was looking into a clear summer day. As for the rest of her, God sure had done a good job taking care of that, as well. And yet, he'd said something to upset or offend her. For the life of him, he couldn't think of what.

Ben realized the neighbor had walked into his house. *No hellos, dude? That's fine. I'd rather you stay away from Maggie, anyway.* He inwardly growled. There he went again. Acting jealous over a woman he barely knew.

Jane placed her hand on Ben's arm. "Hello, Ben. It's good to see you. What brings you over today?"

He glanced at Maggie. She still hadn't looked at him. He dug his mother's check out of his jeans pocket. "Mom wanted me to bring this by. Said she owed you some money."

Jane swatted the air. "I'd forgotten all about that." She took the check from his hand. "Oops. She's ten dollars short."

Ben reached into his back pocket and pulled out his wallet. "Sorry 'bout that. I'll pay—"

Jane cackled and punched his arm. "Gotcha. She paid the right amount. Tell her I said thank you."

He grinned as he shoved the wallet back into his pocket. He should have seen that coming. "I will."

The front door of Jane's house opened, and a blond-haired boy not much older than the twins raced outside. "I'm up, Mommy. I took a good nap."

He wrapped his arms around Maggie's leg, and Ben blinked and took a step back. She looked at Ben and lifted her chin as she picked up the boy and placed him on her hip.

Ben sputtered, "You...you have a son?"

Chapter 4

Maggie stared at Ben, trying to decipher his expression. It irked her that her mind veered toward him so much, and she wondered if she'd traipsed through his thoughts, as well. She wrapped her hand around Petey's chubby wrist. "Ben, this is my son, Petey."

Petey pulled his hand away from hers and waved. "Hi, Ben."

"Mr. Ben," Aunt Jane corrected.

Petey held up three fingers. "I'm free, Mr. Ben." He cackled then clapped.

"Three," Aunt Jane repeated. "Stick your tongue against your teeth. Th-th-three."

Maggie pursed her lips. Her aunt constantly corrected Petey for his slight pronunciation errors. Personally, she found them cute. She winked at her son. "Good job, Petey." She looked at Ben, who still stood speechless. "My big guy's birthday is in a couple weeks, so we've been practicing our age." She tickled Petey's tummy. "Haven't we?"

"I didn't know you were married."

"Actually, I'm a widow. Petey's dad died in Afghanistan."

Her gaze never left Ben's as she put Petey on the ground. Shock and then pity wrapped his features. "I'm sorry," he mumbled.

She nodded. "It's been four years. He didn't even get to meet Petey."

Before Ben could respond, her young son grabbed his hand. "I'll show you my trucks."

Aunt Jane tried to take Petey's hand. "Why don't you show me?"

"No." Petey shook his head and pulled at Ben's hand. "I'll show *you*." He smiled up at him, and Maggie's heart twisted at the sweet expression that enveloped Ben's face.

Aunt Jane tried again. "Pete, Mr. Ben might have other places he needs to go."

"Please." Petey looked up at Ben with wide eyes and a slight pout. Even at his young age, the kid knew that innocent, yet imploring expression worked every time to get his way with Maggie.

"I've got time."

Ben followed Petey into the house, and Maggie bit back a chuckle. The look obviously worked on Ben, as well. Aunt Jane released an exaggerated sigh and shook her head slowly as she made her way behind them.

Maggie furrowed her brows. What was that about? Just moments ago, Aunt Jane had tried to set her up with the neighbor. Her aunt hinted in every conceivable way without actually telling the man to ask Maggie out. She shuddered; thankful Ben had driven up when he did. The neighbor guy kinda gave her the creeps. Not that he seemed physically threatening, just kinda acted like a jerk.

By the time Maggie walked into the house, Petey had already dragged Ben to the bedroom she shared with her son. Her cheeks warmed as she thought about the unmade bed and laundry strewn about the room. Normally, the room was picked-up and clean, but today she planned to wash clothes. *And of course, that's when Petey takes a guest, Ben Jacobs no less, back there.*

Maggie glanced at Aunt Jane, who'd plopped down in her favorite rocking recliner. She took off her wide-brimmed hat and sat it on the end table. Her lips were pursed as she stared down the hall after Ben and Petey. Only moments ago, she'd been teasing the man. Now she acted upset.

"Aunt Jane, is something wrong?"

Her aunt opened her mouth then clasped her lips shut. She shook her head.

Confused and a bit uncomfortable with her aunt's behavior, Maggie walked to the bedroom door, leaned against it and watched as Petey introduced Ben to every single truck he owned. Her heartstrings tugged at Ben's genuine interest in her son as he helped line up the vehicles by size and color. She didn't even mind the messy room so much anymore.

Ben glanced up and grinned at her. "He's a great kid."

Maggie nodded. "I think so."

Petey grabbed Ben's jaw and turned it back to the toys. "And dis one is a dump truck. You put dirt in it."

"This," said Ben, emphasizing the "th" sound.

"Dis!" Petey exclaimed. He handed a couple of his favorites to Ben then stood up and grabbed Ben's hand. "Come on, let's play outside."

"Now, Petey…"

"It's okay." Ben lifted his hand to her. "I've got a little time. I don't mind to play with the little guy." He stood and tousled Petey's hair.

Maggie feared her heart might pound out of her chest as she followed the two of them to the front door. She stopped and looked at her aunt. "You wanna come with us?"

Aunt Jane frowned and shook her head again. She picked up the television remote. "Think I'll just see what shows are on."

Maggie wrinkled her nose. Aunt Jane rarely watched television. "You sure?"

She waved her hand. "I'm sure. You go on."

Maggie joined Ben and Petey on the driveway. Her son found a piece of sidewalk chalk, and Ben drew an elaborate road design. With rocks and weeds the two found alongside the road, in the flower bed and in the lawn, they designed fictitious stores and houses.

Maggie's heart thrilled and broke to pieces at the same time. Petey sucked up the attention. Maggie was mom. She loved him, took care of him, disciplined him. And Aunt Jane filled a different role. She took on teaching him about the world around him. Her son was already beginning to recognize letters, and he loved when Aunt Jane read to him.

But Petey had never had a dad to play with. Someone who would get down in the dirt and think like a boy. Paul would have been a terrific dad. He would have taught Petey everything he ever needed or wanted to know about being a rough-and-tumble little guy. But Paul was gone, and Petey had no idea what he was missing.

Ben looked at his cell phone. "Little buddy, I'm going to have to head home."

Petey's face puckered. Knowing a fit was coming,

Maggie jumped up off the ground and scooped him onto her hip. "Why don't you thank Mr. Ben for playing with you?"

He shook his head, and Maggie's cheeks warmed. Now Ben would get to see her son pitch a full-fledged fit.

"Tell you what, buddy. Why don't you and Mommy and Aunt Jane come to my house for lunch on Sunday?"

Petey perked up.

Maggie said, "We couldn't possibly do that. Your mother—"

"Loves to have visitors." Ben lifted three fingers. "That's three days."

Petey pointed to his chest. "I'm free, too."

Ben nodded at Petey, then looked at her. The intensity in his gaze curled her toes. "Please."

No. Say no. She was too attracted to him. He was too good with her son. She didn't need the distraction of a man. She needed to help Aunt Jane. She needed to get her own life in order. She still missed Paul something fierce.

"Okay," Maggie whispered.

He smiled then jumped into his truck, tossed back one last wave and then drove away. She still felt dizzy as she walked back into the house and shut the door.

"Maggie."

She turned toward her aunt Jane, who had clasped her hands together and pressed them against her lips. "Yes."

"Don't fall for that boy."

"What do you mean?"

Her aunt pursed her lips. "That boy has a lot to deal with on his own. He doesn't need a girlfriend." She looked at Petey. "Or a little boy."

Maggie swallowed. If there was something wrong with Ben, if he was dangerous, she needed to know that. Now.

Her aunt must have read her thoughts as she clicked

her tongue. "Now don't go making up things in your head. He's not a bad boy. He just needs to focus on what's important."

Maggie opened her mouth to ask more, but Aunt Jane lifted her hand. "That's all I'm gonna say."

With his dad's "amen" at the close of the prayer over their dinner, Ben lifted his head and released the hands of his nieces, Emma and Emmy, sitting on each side of him. His mother scooped a spoonful of tossed salad onto her plate then passed it to his brother. Kirk maneuvered the bowl away from Ronald's grasp, while Callie picked up a breadstick, ripped it in half and gave the pieces to the twins.

It wasn't often the whole family could get together for dinner. Finding a chunk of free time with three grown children and four grandchildren proved quite a challenge for his parents. But his dad beamed and his mom smiled incessantly when they had the opportunity to sit around the table as they were doing now.

"Well, girls, I know fall break is next week. What big plans have you made?" asked Mom.

Emma pushed a strand of hair behind her ear. "I'll just be glad to be out of there for a week."

Ben grimaced. Starting middle school had been a challenge for his niece. Lots of new teachers. A change in friends. He remembered struggling through those years and hated to see Emma go through it.

Emmy pouted. Even though she was a year younger than Emma, she was half a head taller and full of chatter. "Not me. I hate missing school."

Their dad, Jack, cleared his throat. "Actually, your mom and I have a surprise for you."

Emmy sat up straighter, while Emma seemed to remain unaffected. Ben had trouble accepting Jack back into the family after his eight-year hiatus due to alcoholism, but he'd been true to Ben's sister and nieces for two years. No falling off the wagon, so to speak, so Ben was beginning to like the guy again.

Pamela grinned and took Jack's hand in hers. Jack might be making his way back into Ben's good graces, but Ben still didn't like seeing Pamela get all starry-eyed over the guy. Jack had been gone a lot longer than he'd been back. And sometimes Ben wished Pamela would remember that.

'Course if Dad could read Ben's thoughts, he'd reprimand him, tell him that Jack had become a Christian and changed his ways. Ben was glad for Jack's relationship with Christ, but he also knew firsthand how tempting an addiction could be.

Ben's dad nodded to his son-in-law. "Well, tell us what you and Pamela have planned."

Jack said, "We're going to Texas for fall break."

"What?" Emmy squealed.

"Really?" Emma's eyes twinkled for the first time all evening.

Pamela placed a piece of lasagna on her plate. "Yep. Your grandpa got airline tickets at a terrific rate. Todd and Kari are already making us an itinerary." She chuckled and looked around the table. "We'll be so exhausted after visiting Jack's family we'll need a vacation from our vacation."

"We're going to ride in an airplane?" Emma gasped, but Ben noted she seemed more thrilled than scared of the idea.

"You'll have so much fun," said Callie. "When do you leave?"

"Saturday," Jack said then took a bite of salad.

The girls gasped and responded in unison. "In two days!"

Ben laughed and tousled their hair. "Sounds like you two will have to get to packing."

"You'll have a great time," said Ben's dad.

"I hate leaving in October," Pamela said, looking from their dad to their mom. "I know it's one of the busiest times of the year."

Mom swatted her hand then pointed to Ben, Kirk and Callie. "Nonsense. We still have your brothers and Callie here. You have fun. If we need help, we'll find someone."

Callie wiped Teddy's face after he tried to shove part of his lasagna noodle up his nose. "Remember, we're going to the Carters' house for a birthday party after church on Sunday, so we won't be here for lunch."

Pamela laughed. "We won't be here, either."

Mom nodded. "I guess Dad and I will have a quiet Sunday afternoon. Ben, what are your plans?"

Ben frowned, realizing he probably should have checked with his family before inviting Jane, Maggie and her son to lunch. He dipped his chin and lifted his shoulders. "Actually, I invited some people to lunch."

"Really?" His dad cocked his head, and Ben's face warmed. "Who?"

"Jane." He took a drink of his iced tea, hoping the cool liquid would halt the blush he knew was overtaking his face. "And Maggie and her son."

Kirk lifted one eyebrow. "Isn't Maggie the gal who just moved here?"

Pamela leaned forward, placed her elbow on the table and plopped her chin on her fist. She batted her eyes as she nodded. "She sure is."

Callie bit her bottom lip. "She's cute, too."

Kirk howled. "Oh, I wish we could be here on Sunday."

Ben clasped his hands under the table, determined to act unaffected by their bantering. "I just thought her son might enjoy the activity center. But since none of you will be here, I'll just call and cancel."

"Nonsense," said his mother. "That little boy of hers will have a terrific time."

His dad agreed. "And I haven't gotten a chance to meet this girl, though I've heard she's working hard at keeping Jane's shop afloat."

His mom looked dismayed. "Not sure how that will be possible."

"No, really, I'll call and cancel," said Ben. "I thought Petey could play with the boys. Meet the girls."

"Petey?" asked Kirk, and Ben bit back a growl at his brother's teasing expression.

"Do not cancel," said his mom. "I insist."

Ben nodded as he shoved a bite of lasagna into his mouth. Trying to ignore his sister's and brother's knowing glances and occasional winks, he decided it was a good thing they'd all be gone this weekend. He didn't know how he felt about Maggie and her son. The kid was amazing, and Maggie set his heart to pounding every time he saw her. But he didn't have anything to offer them. He lived with his brother, worked for his dad and had student-loan debt that would take him years to repay. No, he'd just need to be friends with the woman, and if he kept telling himself that, maybe he'd start to believe it.

Chapter 5

"Mommy, are we going to see Ben and pet animals today?" asked Petey.

Maggie groaned then smiled down at her son. "No, honey. Not today. Mommy's still working." She handed him one of his favorite books and a bag of cheese crackers. "Why don't you read your book?"

"When are we going, Mommy?"

Maggie held up her pointer finger. "One day. We'll go tomorrow. After church."

Petey nodded. "Okay. We'll go after church. Dat's when we go to Ben's house."

Maggie puckered her lips. "Th-th-that."

"D-d-dat."

With a sigh, Maggie smiled down at her son, hoping it was normal for her constantly-talking almost-four-year-old to struggle with sounding out a "th." She also hoped it was normal that the child asked about going to Ben's place at least ten times a day.

It didn't help that she thought about going to Ben's house almost as often. She placed a price sticker on a baby dress that had been donated earlier that morning. Holding up the tiny lime-green-and-white-polka-dotted getup with ruffles adorning the hems and a bright pink flower in the center of the collar, Maggie reminisced about when Petey had been just a small baby. She'd always wanted to have a little sister or two for him. Thinking of Ben again, she sighed and hung up the dress.

The last thing she needed was a man. The shop hadn't had one customer the entire week, unless she counted Ben stopping by the house to pay for some things Tammie had bought a week ago. But she didn't count that. Two ladies had stopped by to drop off items to sell, but neither had even glanced at anything in the consignment shop.

"I think I'm going to have to get a part-time job," she whispered to herself.

"What, Mommy?"

"Nothing, sweetie."

She had no idea what kind of job she could get. She couldn't work just anywhere. She had Petey and Aunt Jane to think about. Maybe there was something she could do at the church, or the pastor might know of a place that would be a good fit for her. She'd enjoyed her aunt's church more than she'd expected. The people were welcoming, and the music and sermons were uplifting. Maggie hadn't realized how much she'd missed being part of a church family.

Petey threw his book on the floor and stood. He puckered his bottom lip. "Mommy, I wanna go see Ben and animals."

The child was like a broken record. She shook her head. "Not today."

His frown deepened, and he furrowed his brows and stomped his foot. "I wanna go today."

"Petey." She started to scold him when the front door opened and the bell jingled. Plastering on a smile, she turned to the front and saw her aunt walking toward her.

Aunt Jane cupped the bottom of her hair with her palm. "What do you think?"

Maggie thought her aunt needed to stop going to the beauty salon every two weeks to get her hair fixed, but she bit back the words. "Your hair looks lovely."

Aunt Jane beamed. "Thanks." She motioned to Petey. "Why don't you and Pete go get some lunch and maybe stop by the park for a little while?"

"I still need to price these." She held up several outfits.

Her aunt shook her head. "I've been running this business since long before you were born. I think I can handle putting a few stickers on some clothes."

"But—"

"No buts. Pete doesn't need to be cooped up in a store all day." Aunt Jane tapped Maggie's cheek. "And neither do you."

Not wanting to argue with her further, and knowing Petey was on the verge of throwing a complete conniption, Maggie gathered their things, took her son's hand and headed out of the shop. Outside, she drank in the perfect October temperature. It was a good day to go to the park, and Petey needed some playtime. "But, God, our bills aren't going to pay themselves," she murmured.

She tried not to think about their precarious financial situation as they walked home and while she and Petey ate lunch.

After they finished eating, she zipped up her son's

jacket, and they made their way out of the house just as Aunt Jane walked up the driveway. Maggie rushed to her. "Is something wrong, Aunt Jane?"

"Nah. Just weren't any customers, so I decided to close her up."

Maggie's jaw dropped, and she fought the urge to wring her sweet aunt's neck. "Aunt Jane, we definitely won't get any customers if the shop is closed."

"They'll come back another time if they want something."

Maggie pursed her lips. It was no wonder her aunt was in so much financial trouble. "We have to pay our bills."

Aunt Jane shook her head. "They always get paid, Maggie. You worry too much."

Before she could respond, her aunt walked into the house. Maggie threw back her head and lifted her gaze to the heavens. "God, what am I supposed to do?"

"I wanna go see Ben and animals," said Petey.

Maggie rolled her eyes and looked down at her son. His expression showed such sweet innocence and sincerity that she couldn't bring herself to scold him. "Tomorrow, Petey. Today we're going to go swing."

"Swing! I love to swing." He pulled her hand toward the sidewalk. "Let's go, Mommy."

They'd just go have a good time together. Since their move, she hadn't spent nearly the time with him that she usually did. Today she wouldn't worry about the consignment shop or Aunt Jane's beauty parlor visits or a part-time job. Today would be about her and Petey.

"But we go see Ben and animals tomorrow, right?" asked Petey.

"So, what do you think about Old Tom?" asked Ben.

Pete reached up and wrapped his arms around the goat's neck. "I love him."

Ben grinned as he gently pried the boy's fingers from the old goat's hair. Tom was no stranger to small children trying to grab at his hair or pet him with more fervor than was probably comfortable. Still, he was getting up in years, and Ben didn't want to take any chances that the old critter would decide to nibble on a few of Pete's fingers.

Ben wrapped his hand around Pete's. "How would you like to see the horses?"

Pete's eyes widened as he nudged Ben forward. Ben scooped the boy into his arms. "You're going the wrong way, little guy." He pointed to the barn.

Maggie fell into step beside him. He tried not to think about how cute she looked in the long-sleeved denim shirt, khaki skirt and brown boots that went up to her knees. Or how he wanted to sweep away the little strands of blond hair that had fallen out of her ponytail and fanned her pink cheeks. Or how her eyes, bluer than the sky above their heads, drew him like the thrill of a good poker hand. Or how her lips reminded him of one of their apples, full and red and ready to be tasted. Or... He ground his teeth together. He had to stop thinking of ors.

He hefted the boy higher on his hip. No, he didn't need to think about Maggie Grant at all.

"How many horses do you have?"

Maggie's voice seemed to blow with the breeze, like a song against his ear. He shook his head. What in the world had gotten into him? He blamed Callie. She'd made him and Kirk watch that ridiculous chick flick last night, and now he was thinking about mushy stuff that men didn't think about. He needed to grab his brother later and toss a few horseshoes, maybe have an arm wrestling match or possibly just go ahead and punch each other a few times to knock the manliness back into him.

For now, he'd just keep his gaze on the barn and the kid. "We have four. If you don't mind, I'll take Pete on a ride."

Pete shouted with excitement, and Ben looked at Maggie, noted the fear in her eyes and wished he'd asked her first. She bit her bottom lip, and Ben found himself biting his, as well. Quickly, he pinched his lips together.

"Will it be safe?" she whispered.

"Well, sure. We'll ride Princess. She's Callie's horse. Broke her leg some years back, and ever since Kirk nursed her back to health, she's been as docile as a newborn foal."

Maggie's brows rose as she pointed to Pete. "That child was not always what I would call *docile* when he was a newborn."

Ben laughed. "He'll be safe. I promise."

Pete was ecstatic when he saw the horses. Ben took him to pet each one then handed Pete to Maggie while he put a saddle on Princess. Heat washed over him as Maggie watched him work. He fumbled with the strap a couple of times and blew his hair off his forehead to try to settle his nerves.

"Would it be safer for you to ride with Pete or to walk beside him?" asked Maggie.

"I wanna ride with Ben!" exclaimed Pete.

"Either way will be fine." Ben placed his foot in the stirrup then righted himself up on the horse. "But I'll ride with him since that's what he wants."

Maggie smiled, and Ben clamped his lips shut to keep from sighing. He was gonna wring Callie's neck the next time she turned on a girlie show. He reached for Pete, and Maggie handed the boy to him. Ben settled him in front then nudged Princess's side. Pete cackled as they walked around a small area in front of the barn. After a bit, Ben hopped down and guided Princess around the yard while Maggie walked alongside to make sure Pete didn't fall off. The little guy protested when Ben led Princess back to the barn. She'd been out long enough, and Ben could tell she was feeling a little anxious.

"Have you ever ridden a horse?" he asked Maggie as she hefted Pete onto her hip. Though the little guy didn't want to admit it, Pete was tuckered out. He almost instantly rested his cheek on her shoulder.

She shook her head. "No. I haven't really been around horses."

"Maybe I could take you riding sometime." Hoping he sounded nonchalant and a huge blush wasn't trailing his face and neck, he coughed, covering his mouth with the back of his hand.

She shrugged and stared at him. "Maybe."

Purposely angling away from her, Ben took off the saddle and placed it on the saddle rack, then put away the rest of the tack.

They walked back to the main house, and by the time they made it to the steps, Pete had fallen asleep. Ben motioned toward Pete. "Would you like to lay him down?"

She shook her head. "It's okay. I'll just hold him." He opened the door, and Maggie walked inside. "My guess is Aunt Jane will be ready to go, anyway."

He hated to break it to her, but the last time her aunt visited, Ben had retired back to Kirk and Callie's long before the woman decided to head back to her house. When they walked into the living room, it was just as he expected. His parents and Jane were sitting around the room and Ben's dad was showing her various antiques he'd picked up on his last excursion. The older lady was enthralled with his finds.

"Aunt Jane, are you about ready to go?" asked Maggie.

Her aunt frowned. "Why, Maggie, Mike just got out an assortment of Coca-Cola relics that he's found."

Maggie pointed to Pete. "I think Petey's ready for a nap."

"You're more than welcome to lay him down here," said his mother.

"Yes, do that," insisted Jane.

"But, Aunt Jane…"

"Put the boy to bed, Maggie."

Ben noted the frustration wrapping Maggie's features and motioned for her to follow him. He led her into a bedroom and unfolded the top covers. Maggie lowered Pete onto the bed. He sat up, wiped his eyes and cried out. Noting the slump of her shoulders, Ben reached down and patted Pete's back. "It's time to rest now. Lie down."

Pete sniffled then laid his head on the pillow and scrunched a corner of the sheet into his fist.

Maggie sighed. "Everyone seems to be able to make that child sleep but me."

"Kids are always hardest on their mothers."

Maggie stared up at him and offered a slow smile. "Thanks."

As they walked back into the living room, Ben tried to think of an excuse to invite Maggie to take a walk with him without sounding as if he wanted to spend time alone with her. Maybe he could ask if she wanted to pick some apples or look for a pumpkin. But she sat down on the couch before he got a chance.

"Jane was telling me that you're looking for part-time work," his mother said to Maggie.

She nodded. "I'm going to have to find something."

"How would you like to work here?"

Maggie sat up straight. "Doing what kind of work?"

"Well, a variety of things. Some cleaning of the B and B,

helping when we have crowds at the activity center and the petting zoo, possibly working in the gift shop," said his mom.

"That's a great idea," added his dad. "We could schedule your hours to fit with Jane's and Pete's needs."

Maggie's smile grew wider than Ben had ever seen, and her eyes twinkled with excitement. "That would be great."

Ben's heart drummed in his chest. He would have the opportunity to spend a lot of time with Maggie, and *that* would be great.

At least, he hoped spending time with her would be great.

Chapter 6

Maggie hoped working at the Jacobs Family Farm would be a good thing. Pete chattered constantly about Ben, and when her son wasn't talking about him, she was thinking about the guy. Aunt Jane's warning before she left that Maggie stay focused on the job and not any distractions sent her into even more of a quandary. If there was something wrong with Ben, why wouldn't her aunt just come out and say it?

Once again, Aunt Jane hinted that Maggie should talk to the neighbor guy, which only made her doubt her aunt's ability to judge character. The guy reeked of dishonesty and cowardice, so different from Paul, who'd always exhibited integrity and strength. Ben's face drifted to her mind, and she scratched her head. *I can't think that way about Ben. I barely know him.*

She thought of him showing Petey the animals and taking him for a ride on the horse. She remembered how attentive he was to his parents, his mom especially, always willing to help her when she needed it. Everything she'd seen in Ben showed integrity and strength. Characteristics she wanted Petey to be around.

She parked the car and walked to the B and B. Now was not the time to worry about men. She needed to work. Tammie met her at the door with a smile. "Come in. Let's talk about hours and pay. Then I'll show you around."

Maggie followed Tammie to the kitchen and accepted a glass of iced tea from her new employer. Tammie suggested a schedule that coincided with the hours Maggie wouldn't have to be at the consignment shop. Then she mentioned the pay, and Maggie almost choked on the tea. "Tammie, that's too much."

Tammie grinned. "You might not think so when you see all the work I'm going to have you doing. Come on. I'll show you what I'd like you to do.

Maggie followed her through the B and B. Each bedroom sported some kind of color scheme and looked meticulously clean, as did the bathrooms. "I'm going to have you clean all the areas where our guests stay. I'm really picky, so it won't be an easy task."

"Not afraid of a little elbow grease." Maggie lifted her arm and made a muscle. "Seriously though, these rooms are beautiful."

Tammie laughed. "Thanks, but we're not done yet."

Maggie followed Tammie on a tour of the grounds. She'd already visited the activity center and petting zoo and a lot of the orchard, but she hadn't gone to the café or the gift shop. She listened as Tammie gave her instructions about taking inventory, pricing foods and items and running the register.

"There's so much to take care of," Maggie said as they walked back outside.

"Which is why it takes the whole family to run it," said Tammie.

Maggie looked around the farm. The B and B was the largest house, but two other homes were built on the property, as well as a small cabin that sat a little ways behind the main house. She pointed to the newer two-story, white home. "Is that Pamela and Jack's house?"

"Very soon," Tammie said. "A little more electrical work has to be completed, and the house has to go through an inspection, but they should be able to move in by Thanksgiving."

"That's great."

"Ben will be glad, because he'll be able to move into the cabin." She chuckled. "I think living with the twins is wearing him out."

Maggie shifted her weight from one foot to the other. "I thought Ben liked being around kids. He seems so good with Petey."

"Oh, he's the best with kids." She smacked her hand to her thigh. "Doesn't mean he's ready for them full-time, though."

Maggie tried not to respond to what felt like a punch in the gut. If he wasn't ready for kids, then he wasn't right for her. No questions asked. "So, you want me to start tomorrow?"

"Sounds like a good day to me." Tammie snapped her fingers. "You've met the whole family, right?"

"Everyone except your daughter and her family."

Tammie nodded. "Okay. They won't be back until this weekend, so we'll make sure you all get introduced then. You know if you ever want to bring Pete, we could work it out so he and the boys could play."

"That would be fun for him."

Maggie saw a lone figure walking toward them. Ben.

Knowing she didn't need to spend any more time with him than was necessary, she offered a quick goodbye to Tammie and walked to her car. As she pulled out of the driveway, she blew out a long breath. "God, I've got Aunt Jane who disapproves of Ben for some reason, and now Tammie tells me he's not ready for full-time fatherhood. So why is it I can't stop thinking about him?"

God didn't respond, not that she expected Him to speak out loud or write words across the sky, but she'd still like to feel some kind of peace in her heart. How could she possibly work with that man four out of seven days a week, see him at church on Sundays and still stay away from him? For Petey's sake, she'd have to stay strong.

And use evasive tactics.

Ben walked up to his mom and pointed toward the woman in the economy car driving quickly away from the farm. "Wasn't that Maggie?"

His mom nodded. "We just finished discussing her work here. She's such a sweet woman. I think she'll do a great job."

"Left kinda fast, didn't she?"

"She did." His mom shrugged. "Probably had to pick up Pete." She motioned toward the house. "Come on. Let's get you some lunch. I know you're starving."

He patted his stomach. "You're right about that."

As he walked beside his mom to the house, he looked at the now-empty road. Why hadn't she at least said hello to him? She had to have seen him heading straight for them. He'd been looking forward to seeing her all morning. Hoped he'd get the chance to take her for a horseback ride, or maybe even take her on a tour of the farm. He thought about her and Pete from sunup to sundown, and even some of the time before and after. She must have had somewhere to go in a hurry. He shouldn't read too much into it.

"So, do we have any word on the actual date when Pamela and Jack's house will be finished?" he asked.

His mom grinned as they made their way into the house. She opened the refrigerator and handed him the lettuce and tomato. "Anxious to move, are you?"

He took a knife out of the drawer and cut the tomato into slices. "I'm sure Kirk and Callie would like to have their house to themselves, as well."

She placed slices of bread on plates then topped them with ham. "Within a month. No definite date, but not too much longer."

Ben put the toppings on the sandwiches then added potato chips and a pickle to his plate. He wasn't exactly thrilled with the idea of moving into the cabin, but it would be better than living with his brother and sister-in-law.

His phone vibrated in his pocket. He pulled it out and looked at Taylor's name on the screen. Pointing to the door, he said, "I'll be right back."

His mom grinned. "Possible job?"

He wished. He shook his head. "Just a friend."

A shadow fell over his mom's expression, but she didn't say anything. He stepped outside then answered the call. "Hi, Taylor."

"Hey, man. If I didn't know any better, I'd think you were trying to avoid me."

Ben scratched at the stubble already forming on his shaven jaw. "Yeah. I've been busy."

"Got a game going tonight."

Ben blew out a long breath. "Taylor, I've told you I'm not playing anymore."

Surprise filled him at how easy the words fell from his lips. Since meeting Maggie and Pete, he'd felt like he had a new purpose, something to look forward to. Even though the woman had never once said she was interested in him, and she'd raced out of here without so much as a wave less than an hour ago. Still, he hoped, and even prayed, there could be something more than just friendship between him and Maggie. As cliché as the statement sounded, he understood Tom Cruise's quote in *Jerry Maguire,* when he told Renée Zellweger she made him want to be a better man. Ever since he'd met Maggie and Pete, Ben wanted to be a better man.

"Come on, man. You had a few bad games, but Lady Luck is a fickle gal. You might be back in her good graces. How will you know unless you play?" said Taylor.

"Sorry, man. I gotta go. Gonna eat lunch then get back to work."

"On the farm," Taylor chided.

"Yep. Talk to you later." Ben ended the call, fighting off the nick to his pride at Taylor's snide tone. His friend knew Ben felt like a failure having to run home to Mom and Dad because he couldn't find a job.

He walked back into the house to find his mom and dad sitting at the kitchen table eating lunch. They exchanged a concerned glance with each other. He hated those looks.

"Was that a friend from school?" asked his dad.

Ben sighed. In his heart, he knew he shouldn't be so frustrated with his parents' concern. He'd given them reason to worry. But he wanted to be treated as a grown man. He wasn't gambling. Hadn't gambled in months. "Yep. He wanted me to join him for a poker game tonight."

His mom dipped her head and looked down at her

plate. Dad stared into his eyes, determined to see to his core. "Well," said Dad, "what did you say?"

"I said I don't play anymore." He took a drink of his iced tea. "I haven't even really had the urge as much lately."

His mom looked up at him. "I'm so glad, son."

"Just have to stay away from temptation. That's the key," said his dad.

"And stay focused on God," added his mother.

"That's a given," said Dad.

"Well, I'm planning to do that," said Ben. He finished his lunch then excused himself. Before he headed back to the farm, he wanted to check on possible job openings. He turned on the computer and skimmed the job-posting website he'd joined. One new electrical engineering opening.

He logged on to the company's website and read through their mission statement and goals for the future. He sent a quick email to the human resources director, introducing himself and requesting that she check out his résumé online. With more work to do on the farm, he got off the computer but didn't get up. His heart felt heavy and hopeful at the same time.

Bowing his head, he closed his eyes. "God, I want to be a different man. I want to find a position using my electrical engineering degree, but I don't want to fall back into gambling. Help me."

He opened his eyes and rubbed his hands together. "And, God, I'd like to get to know Maggie better. Amen."

Standing, he smiled at the contentment that filled his heart. It felt good to be talking with God again.

Chapter 7

Maggie put away the cleaning supplies in the laundry room. She'd finished cleaning the B and B. As soon as she picked up and took out the trash at the activity center, she'd be ready to head home. She brushed stray hairs away from her forehead with the back of her hand. Tammie had been right about the work being harder than she'd expected, but she'd still enjoyed herself, and the extra income would go a long way in helping to get Aunt Jane back on her feet.

She walked outside and breathed in the fresh country air. The trees, swathed in orange, yellow, red and salmon-colored leaves, covered the mountains behind the farm. The orchard boasted ripened apples and the pumpkin patch showed large, round fruit. She missed the convenience of the city, but she couldn't help but sigh in awe at the beauty and majesty of God's creation.

After picking up wrappers and wadded napkins left

on the tables and all around the activity center, she sat
in one of the swings facing the mountains. She felt as if
she spent every moment of her life worried about money
or taking care of Petey. How long had it been since she'd
allowed herself to just sit and be quiet?

She couldn't remember the last time she'd spent true
one-on-one time with God, either. But now, looking at
the majestic warm colors rising and falling like waves
on those mountains and knowing that God had painted
that picture, Maggie's spirit spilled over with praise. *God,
You are amazing. Your design of this world is perfect.*

Those first months after Paul passed away, a friend
had encouraged her to wake up every day praising God
for everything she could think of. Her friend promised
that praise would help heal her heart, and it had. But
lately, she'd forgotten.

Pushing the ground with her feet, she started to swing
slowly. "God, You are awe-inspiring. Your creation is
breathtaking." With each utterance of praise, she pumped
her legs harder until she was swinging as she had as
a child. She pulled out the ponytail band and allowed
her hair to flow freely. The wind felt glorious whipping
through her hair.

"Having fun?"

Maggie startled at Ben's voice. She looked to the side
and saw him leaning against the swing's pole, one leg
crossed in front of the other and his arms crossed in front
of his chest. Noting the settled position, she wondered
how long he'd been watching her, and she tried to remember if she'd actually spoken any of her thoughts aloud.

"The mountains are beautiful to look at," he said.

She pinched her lips together. So she had been utter-
ing her praises aloud. Warmth washed over her, and she
couldn't decide if she should stop swinging and risk him

seeing her embarrassment. Realizing he might think she was playing on the job, she stopped abruptly and begged God to make the blush that she knew was spreading over her face and neck go away.

"I'm finished working for the day." She slipped on her shoes. Her face warmed again as she pointed to the swing. "I hadn't done that in years. Just thought I'd take a minute—"

"When was the last time you went down a slide?" Ben pointed to the mammoth yellow slide. His eyes twinkled with delight, and she knew he wasn't making fun of her.

She grinned. "It's been a few years."

He lifted his brows. "You wanna?"

She shook her head.

"Oh, come on."

He took her hand, and Maggie's heartbeat skipped as he guided her to the slide.

"I'll go first."

He released her hand and Maggie made a fist. She was as bad as a middle-school girl with her heart fluttering because he'd held her hand for all of a couple of seconds. He scaled the steps then waved to her from the top. With a loud yell, he slid down the slide then jumped to his feet. "See. It's fun."

Still embarrassed, Maggie looked around the farm. "Where is everyone?"

"Mom and Dad are probably having lunch. Jack and Pamela and the girls are in Texas visiting his family. Kirk and Callie took the boys for a checkup." He walked over to her, leaned down until his lips were mere inches from her ear and whispered, "No one will see you."

A chill washed over her and she chuckled, hoping he couldn't see how his nearness affected her. "Okay."

She made her way up the slide and slid down. Excitement raced through her as she thought of how much she'd enjoyed playing at the park as a girl. No worries. No real problems. Just play.

Ben grabbed her hands. "Come on. We'll race."

She followed him up the steps. He sat on one side of the slide, and she sat on the other. At his "GO," they raced down the slide. Reaching the bottom first, Maggie doubled over in laughter. He joined her, and she had to fight off the urge to wrap her arms around him.

He must have read her thoughts, because he cleared his throat then guided her to the merry-go-round. She jumped on and he spun her around. Dizzy, but refreshed, Maggie soon hopped off. She placed her hands on her hips. "That was so much fun. I haven't done anything like that in forever."

"Me, neither." Ben's stomach growled and he pressed his hand against it. "I think it's time for lunch. You wanna join me?"

Maggie would have loved to, but she shook her head. "No. I need to get back to the house. Aunt Jane has had Petey all morning."

"You should bring him back to the farm sometime."

Maggie bit her bottom lip, remembering Tammie's saying that Ben enjoyed his nephews but didn't want to be a father full-time. Petey adored Ben. He still talked about him constantly. Inwardly, she berated herself. He wasn't asking her to date him, just said she should bring him back to the farm. "I will sometime. He loves it here."

Ben gazed at her for several seconds, and Maggie knew she should look away, but she couldn't. Something about the man drew her.

"Maggie, would you be willing to go to dinner with me?"

Say no. Aunt Jane has warned you to be careful. His

mom said he doesn't want kids right now. Think with your mind, not your heart. "Sure."

Ben settled Pete onto the movie theater booster seat between himself and Maggie.

"I never been to a movie, Mr. Ben," said Pete.

"And he might not make it all the way through," said Maggie.

Ben shrugged. "Wouldn't be surprised if he didn't."

"I'm sitting between you and Mommy."

Ben settled into his seat, putting his soft drink in the holder away from Pete. He handed the boy his kid's box containing a bag of gummies, a small popcorn and a capped lemon-lime soft drink. "Yes, you are."

Maggie leaned toward Pete. "Remember, we talked about how we're supposed to be quiet in a movie so that everyone can hear."

As children of all sizes and age ranges settled in around them to watch the newest animated release, Ben grinned over Pete's head at Maggie and mouthed, "I don't know that it will matter."

She giggled, and Ben's heart fluttered. He enjoyed spending time with her and Pete. He smiled each time he thought about their time playing at the activity center. Sure, he'd wanted this date to be just the two of them, but Pete was one of the neatest kids he'd met. And if Ben wanted to get closer to Maggie, Pete was part of the deal. *And I'm okay with that.*

The lights dimmed, and Pete gasped and grabbed Ben's hand. Ben pointed to the big screen. "That means it's almost time for the movie to start."

Pete held his hand tight through the first few commercials, but soon released his grip, grabbed a gummy worm and shoved half of it into his mouth. Maggie might be surprised to know Ben had spent many an hour watching animated princess movies when his nieces were younger. He kind of felt good knowing he'd been with Pete for his first-ever movie trip.

The movie started, and Pete was enraptured. For about thirty minutes. Then he had to go to the bathroom. Ben helped him, washed his hands then escorted him back. Fifteen minutes later, Pete spilled his soft drink on his shirt. After the removal of the shirt, a patting down with tissues and a quick muffled cry, Pete was engrossed in the movie again. Until he had to go to the bathroom again. By the time the movie ended, Ben had no idea what the story had been about, and he didn't care one bit because Pete beamed with excitement that he'd been to his first movie.

They walked back to the car, and Maggie put Pete in his booster car seat. She stood and looked at Ben over the hood of the car. Wrinkling her nose, she said, "Not what you expected, huh?"

Ben chuckled. "That was exactly what I expected. I haven't forgotten taking Emma and Emmy to the movies when they were small."

Maggie cocked her head and stared at him. "You didn't mind?"

He frowned. "Why would I mind? I enjoy spending time with Pete. He's great."

"I thought…"

"What?"

"Well…" She swatted her hand through the air. "Never mind."

Before he could question her, she got into the passenger's seat. He got in and started the car, knowing he'd ask what she meant later. Smiling at Pete through the rearview mirror, he said, "You wanna get a hamburger?"

The boy hollered an affirmative, and Ben drove to

a nearby fast-food restaurant. Once they'd gotten their food, Ben watched as Maggie took care of her son. She was such a beautiful woman and a terrific mother. Though a bit premature in the relationship, he wished he had more to offer. He wouldn't date a woman with a child simply for the fun of it. If he didn't think there was a possible future, he'd never even ask her on a date. But he did like Maggie. Liked her a lot. He wished he had a job. He wished he didn't have all his debt.

"Penny for your thoughts," said Maggie.

He looked up at her, not realizing he'd been staring at Pete. "Just thinking about what a good mom you are."

Her cheeks flushed, and Ben wanted to trace his finger down the side of her jaw. She didn't say anything, just took a drink of her Coke. He ate the last bite of his hamburger then cleaned up their wrappers and threw them away. Pete talked about the movie the whole way home and would hardly give Maggie time to get him out of the car seat before he was running into the house to tell Aunt Jane about their time together.

Ben unbuckled the car seat from his backseat and put it in Maggie's car. When he turned toward her, she stood gripping the strap of her purse. "Ben, I need to talk to you."

He frowned. "Sure."

"Look. I shouldn't have agreed to the date. I have Petey to think about."

"I like Pete. A lot."

"I know, but Petey's full-time. He's number one. I can't date a man who doesn't understand…"

Ben reached out and took Maggie's hand in his. She clamped her lips shut, and he traced his thumb along the top of her hand. "I know that. I adore children. I probably want more kids than a wife would be willing to have. I wouldn't have asked you out if I didn't understand you're a two-person package."

She lowered her gaze. "Oh."

With his hand, he lifted her chin until their gazes met. "That's not to say that I wouldn't also like to spend time just you and me."

Maggie smiled. "I'd like that, too."

"You wanna try this again?"

She nodded, and Ben leaned down and kissed the top of her head. He was glad she was willing because he had a feeling she already owned his heart.

Chapter 8

The past few weeks had been one stress piled on top of another for Maggie. The day after their movie date with Ben, Petey came down with a stomach virus, which he then shared with her and Aunt Jane. Maggie's illness seemed to linger the longest probably because she tried to keep the consignment store open, and she refused to miss more than one day of work at the Jacobs Farm. By the time she'd fully recovered the bills were due, and they'd received almost no income from the shop. She barely put together enough to pay the bills.

She tried again to tighten a stripped screw on the large tricycle she'd bought from the consignment store for Petey's fourth birthday. Knowing the thing wouldn't last through the next summer, she'd wanted Petey to have a better present, but she couldn't do anything about the dilapidated toy. She had to have a gift for Petey, and the tricycle was all she could afford.

The buzzer on the stove sounded. She raced into the kitchen and opened the oven door. Smoke billowed out, making her cough. She fanned the air and bit back tears as she pulled out the blackened cake. *Think, Maggie. How can you fix this?*

She glided a butter knife along the sides of the cake then flipped the pan upside down onto the cookie sheet. The cake dropped out, and she lifted off the pan to find a chunk from the center had stuck to the bottom. Fuming at the gaping hole in the baked good, she threw back her head. "I am the world's worst cake baker."

She should have let the cake cool for ten minutes before taking it out of the pan. Anyone with any sense would know that. She glanced at the clock. Aunt Jane would be home with Petey in half an hour. Panic swelled within her. She was running out of time.

The doorbell rang, and Maggie decided to ignore it. She took out the red plates and napkins then got the icing, candles and sprinkles from the cabinet. *How in the world am I going to fix the gaping hole in the middle of the cake?*

The doorbell rang again, and she released an exaggerated sigh. Stomping to the front door, she peeked through the peephole and saw Ben. Ugh. She wished they hadn't invited him. But what choice did she have? Petey chattered about the man off and on every day. Forcing a smile to her lips, she opened the door. "You might not want to come in here. I'm creating a disaster that—"

She gasped when she saw the brand-new bicycle with training wheels in Ben's hand. He lifted it. "Present for the birthday boy."

Covering her mouth with her palms, she couldn't stop

the single tear that streamed down her cheek. "How did you know?"

"You mentioned it to Mom. She mentioned it to me."

She furrowed her brows. "But, you got him a bike?"

"Maggie, the boy is going to be four." He lifted four fingers then pointed toward the tricycle. "Much too old for three wheels."

She cocked her head. "That bike has four wheels."

He winked. "Not for long, I'm sure. That kiddo's a quick learner."

Maggie couldn't stop herself. She didn't even want to. She wrapped her arms around him, relishing his musky scent, the strength of his arm around her back and the sweet kindness of the man. "Thank you so much. He's going to love it."

She released him then averted her gaze when she saw the look of longing in his eyes. Motioning him inside, they hid the present in the bedroom then she pointed to the mess on the kitchen table. "Maybe you can help me figure a way to save the cake."

She showed him the rectangular cake that was charred on the bottom and missing a big chunk on the top. She frowned. "I was going to try to put the piece back on top." She pointed to a pile of crumbs on the table. "Didn't work."

He laughed. "Cake's a little dry, isn't it?"

Maggie punched his arm. "I never claimed to be a baker."

He shook his head. "No. You better never do that."

"Hey." She puckered her lips, pretending to be upset. "At least you're cute. You've got that going for you."

"Ben."

He lifted his hands. "Okay. Okay. Well, I could run to the store and pick up a cake."

She shook her head. "No time. Aunt Jane and Petey will be back in twenty minutes or so."

He cupped his chin with his hand, and Maggie tried not to think about how rugged and handsome he looked with stubble tracing his jaw. He snapped his fingers. "I've got an idea."

While Maggie iced the cake, Ben painted a Styrofoam ball to look like a basketball. After using a hair dryer to get the paint to dry quickly, Ben placed the ball in the hole in the center of the cake then Maggie drew some jagged designs around the base of the ball with colored glaze. They stepped back to look at it.

"Well, it won't win any awards," said Ben.

"But it's much better than anything I'd have come up with by myself." The front door opened, and she grinned at Ben. "And just in time."

Petey raced into the kitchen wearing a pointed birthday hat that Aunt Jane must have found somewhere. "Happy birday to me!" He saw Ben and squealed as he wrapped his arms around Ben's legs.

Ben scooped him into his arms. "Happy birthday, big boy. How old are you?"

Petey lifted four fingers. "I'm four."

Ben high-fived him. "You're growing into quite a big man."

Maggie's heart melted—until she saw her aunt's scowl as she walked into the kitchen. "Smells burnt in here."

"Yeah, I'm not the best baker," said Maggie. She pointed to Ben. "But he saved the day with a great idea."

They showed Petey his cake, and the boy cackled with delight when Maggie lit the candles. They sang the "happy birthday" song then Petey blew the candles out. Thankfully, the cake didn't taste as bad as it looked, even though she did suggest no one eat the bottom.

When they finished eating, Maggie brought the bike out of the bedroom, and Petey squealed again. He jumped on it and drove right into a table. Maggie lifted him off. "We'd better take it outside before you break something."

"I have a little present for him, as well," said Ben.

He walked into the living room and brought back a wrapped box. She'd been so worried about the cake, she must not have noticed it. Petey ripped through the wrapping paper and opened the lid. There sat a white cowboy hat just Petey's size.

"Wow." Petey took it out of the box and put it on his head.

Ben tightened the string. "Now you'll have a real cowboy hat to wear the next time you ride Princess."

Petey gave Ben a hug. "Fanks, Mr. Ben."

They walked outside so that Petey could practice riding his bike. Maggie noticed Aunt Jane didn't follow them, but she figured the older woman just didn't want to come back outside after spending the morning with Petey. She took Ben's hand in hers and squeezed. "You're too good to us, Ben."

"That isn't possible." He held tight, and she found she didn't want him to let go.

Ben pushed down jealousy as he watched his parents, Kirk and Callie, and Jack and Pamela drive down the road. After all, he was the one who volunteered to babysit the kids while they went out to eat as couples. Even so, part of him wished he and Maggie could join them.

He thought of her crumbling cake and the twinkle in her eyes when he came up with the idea to place the painted Styrofoam ball in the middle. They still hadn't been able to go on a date, just the two of them. He hoped they could soon. He loved everything he knew about her, except maybe her baking abilities.

"Uncle Ben, Teddy's got a surprise for you," shouted Emmy.

"I'm not changing him," said Emma.

Of course the boys would start dirtying diapers as soon as their parents left. Without a doubt if Teddy made a mess, Ronald would soon follow. "Don't worry, girls. I wouldn't do that to you."

Emma huffed. "Wish we could say the same thing for Mom. If she's watching the boys, we always do diaper duty."

Ben laughed as he scooped Teddy up off the floor. The toddler squalled, not wanting to stop dancing in front of his favorite children's show on television. He wrinkled his nose and tilted back his head. "Don't worry, buddy. I'll move fast."

Once Ben finished with Teddy's diaper, just as he'd predicted, he had to change Ronald's, as well. After washing his hands, he checked on the girls in the dining room.

"Uncle Ben, you wanna play Monopoly?" asked Emmy.

"I remember when you girls were obsessed with Candyland."

Emma snorted. "We wouldn't be playing Monopoly if Mom hadn't made us put away our phones so we'd help you with the twins."

Ben laughed. "I hate to admit it, but my sister is a smart woman. However, I can't play. I'm going to warm up dinner first."

"What are we having?" asked Emmy.

He opened the refrigerator door and pulled back the aluminum foil from the dish Callie left for them. "Looks like baked spaghetti."

"Is she trying to torture us?" asked Emma.

"The boys will be covered in spaghetti sauce," Emmy agreed.

Ben thought the same thing as he placed the tray in the oven. And yet, he knew the boys loved the stuff, so they'd eat well. He took out garlic bread and put it in the oven beside the dish. After taking a quick peek at the twins, who still stood in front of the television dancing to their favorite show, he opened the cabinet and saw the tray of brownies Pamela had made. He thought of Maggie's cake again and chuckled. At least his sister could bake.

"Girls, watch the boys a second. I'm going to check my email."

"Okay," said Emma.

He went into his room and logged on to the computer. He still hadn't heard from the engineering firm. Placing his elbows on the desk, he clasped his hands and rested his chin on them. He thought he should have heard from them by now.

Exhaling a sigh of frustration, he logged on to the job-search website. No new postings. Sure, he could apply for a job in Alabama, and there was one available in Mississippi, but he didn't want to move that far away. He wondered if Maggie would be willing to move. She'd made a huge change once; possibly she'd do it again.

He shook his head. He didn't need to be thinking that far ahead. Not yet, anyway. Besides, he didn't want to apply for any of those positions, anyway. Shutting his computer, he lifted a quick prayer to God. *Show me Your will for me, Lord.*

He walked back into the kitchen as the timer dinged that the food had warmed. After filling the boys' and his plates, he waited for the girls to join him at the table. He offered a quick prayer, and they started to eat.

He grinned as Teddy missed his mouth and shoved

spaghetti in his nose. Moving away from these kiddos wasn't an option he was willing to consider. Unless God called him to it, and right now, he didn't feel that way.

He looked across the table at the girls. "You haven't told me about your trip. How was Texas?"

Emma grinned. "Well, Grandpa bought both of us a new outfit for school."

"Kari bought each of us a necklace." Emmy pulled the small chain away from her neck, and Ben noticed a dainty cross.

"It's very pretty."

"It was good to see them," said Emma.

"Yeah," said Emmy.

Ben took a bite of spaghetti. "It's hard being so far away, huh?"

Emmy nodded. "Kari fixed our hair in these really cool braids."

"Yeah," said Emma. "I wish she could do that all the time."

"Mo'," screeched Ronald.

Ben looked at his plate to see the little guy had swallowed down his whole plate of food. When he got up to get some more, he realized much of the food hadn't actually made it into his mouth, but had fallen beside the high chair. He put the plate in front of his nephew then pulled off two pieces of breadstick to give to the boys.

No. He couldn't leave his nieces and nephews. As hard as it was to wait to get a job that would utilize his degree, the thought of moving away from his family was even harder. Waiting was miserable, and he wanted to be able to pay off bigger chunks of his debt. But there wasn't anything he could do about it. He'd have to be patient.

Chapter 9

Maggie handed the woman her purchase and thanked her for stopping by Jane's Treasures. Sales had picked up a bit with Christmas only a little over a month away, but the gains hadn't been enough. Aunt Jane had returned home from the beauty parlor an hour ago, which frustrated Maggie no end.

She wanted to help her aunt, and she'd hoped the move would prove a new start for her and Petey. Maggie's intentions had been good. She'd planned to take over the consignment store and keep it in the family, possibly even buy the house from Aunt Jane when she could no longer care for it. But her aunt seemed to have her own plans in mind. Or maybe lack of plans. If something didn't happen soon, they'd have to sell the house and shop.

God, I know Aunt Jane doesn't want that. She says she's fine with selling, but only because she doesn't believe there's any other way.

Maggie physically hurt from her lack of peace. Her head ached, her heart palpitated intermittently and she'd had a lot of trouble sleeping at night. No matter how often she prayed, lately God seemed to stay far from her.

She enjoyed the church services, and she'd even started reading her Bible and praying again. And she had moments of contentment, like when she worked on the Jacobs's farm or when she spent time with Ben. But every time she opened the bank account or walked into the consignment store, she became frazzled all over again.

Pushing her aggravation aside, she walked to the rack and reorganized a few of the outfits that had been placed out of order by a customer. The bell above the door rang, and Maggie smiled at the nice-looking man who walked inside. He wore a dark gray business suit and a pink paisley tie, giving him a kind, approachable appearance.

She nodded. "Hello. May I help you find anything?"

He extended his hand, and as Maggie shook it, she noticed he had very nice green eyes, calm and gentle-looking.

"Actually, your aunt sent me to speak with you."

Maggie held her breath. Oh, boy. Another matchmaking session.

The man continued. "I'm Carl Pearson. I'm opening a new insurance agency in town, and I'm looking for a place to buy."

Maggie's heart sank. Why had Aunt Jane sent this guy? Didn't she have faith that Maggie would find a way to keep the business that had been in the family for years? "I'm not sure how I can help you."

Carl Pearson's eyebrows met in a straight line as he looked around the room. "But I thought…"

The front door opened again, and Aunt Jane walked in. She smiled at them then took Mr. Pearson's arm. "I'm sorry I wasn't here when you arrived. I planned to introduce the two of you." She motioned from Maggie to Carl. "Maggie Grant, this is Carl Pearson."

"We've met," Maggie mumbled.

"Wonderful," Aunt Jane said then looked back at the man. "Mr. Pearson, allow me to show you around."

"Call me Carl," he said as he followed her aunt into the back room where Petey played with puzzles.

"Aunt Jane, Mommy and I saw that mouse again," Petey exclaimed.

Maggie placed her hand over her mouth to keep from laughing out loud. That was the last thing her aunt would want a potential buyer to hear.

She couldn't hear all they said, but she did hear her son exclaim from near the restroom, "You gotta flush two times or it don't work."

Maggie's heart flipped with delight. She wanted to race into the back room and cheer on her four-year-old as he told Mr. Carl Pearson all the things that were wrong with the consignment store. He and her aunt walked back into the main room, and Maggie sat up straighter so as not to appear to have been eavesdropping.

"So when can I see the house?" asked the man.

"The…the house?" Maggie stammered.

Aunt Jane waved her hand in the direction of their home next door. "Well, it's not ready for viewing just yet. Possibly my niece and I could have it ready in a week or two."

A week or two? Thanksgiving was in a week. She didn't want to have to stress about getting the house ready to sell during the holidays. In fact, she didn't want to sell it at all. "Aunt Jane, we haven't discussed this."

Her aunt nodded. "Yes, we have."

Maggie frowned. No, they hadn't. Maybe her aunt

was having more trouble than just leaving the pots and pans in odd places in the house. The thought troubled Maggie, and she knew it was something she'd have to tell her mom about.

"I'm not in a big hurry," said Carl, with emphasis on the word *big*. "I wouldn't mind if we waited until after Thanksgiving. However, I would like to view it before Christmas."

"That shouldn't be a problem," said her aunt.

Maggie chewed the inside of her lip, begging God for the words to say to stop her aunt from setting up a time for this man to view their home. She couldn't even call her mom or sister to back her up, because they wanted Aunt Jane to move closer to them.

"Carl, I did introduce you to my niece, didn't I?" simpered Aunt Jane.

Oh, no. Maggie had to think of something and quick. That was her aunt's matchmaking tone.

"She's a fine young lady. Moved all the way from Texas to take care of her old aunt." She placed her hand on Carl's. "You see her husband was in the military. Passed away four years ago."

Carl looked at Maggie, true sympathy filling his expression. "I'm so sorry. My father passed away in Desert Storm."

Maggie nodded. "I'm sorry for you, as well."

"It was very hard."

Maggie swallowed, having not expected the man to be as kind and sincere as he was. Petey yelled from the other room. She excused herself and helped him fit a puzzle piece into its place. When she walked back into the main room, her aunt and Carl Pearson had left. On the counter was a business card with his phone number circled. At the bottom, he'd written, "Call me if you'd like."

* * *

Ben settled into the pew and wrapped his arm around his younger niece. The church's Thanksgiving service was his favorite of the entire year. His family spread out over two pews. Kirk and Callie even brought the twins into the service, though Ben wondered how long they would last.

"After I say a quick prayer, we'll start the service with some special music from the Pope family."

Ben bowed his head and closed his eyes while Pastor Kent prayed. While the Popes took the stage, Ben searched for Maggie. He'd expected Pete to want to sit with them. As if reading his mind, he spotted the boy holding his mom's hand in the back of the sanctuary and pointing at him with his free hand. Ben waved, and Pete broke free of her grasp and ran for him. *I'm not sure that kid knows how to walk.*

Emmy scooted down, and Maggie and Jane slipped into the pew beside him. Pete sat on his lap with his head cocked to one side, listening intently to the Popes' song of praise. Afterward, a young teenager took the stage, then a husband and wife duo. By the time the singing had ended, Ben's heart was already filled to the brim with worship and praise.

Pastor Kent stood among the congregation with a portable microphone. "At this time does anyone wish to share something they are thankful to God for?"

Ben listened as people praised God for the Bible, for their relationship with Him and for their families. As he expected, his mom stood and thanked the Lord for their family. His father followed her, echoing what she'd said.

Callie reached for the microphone then handed Teddy to Dad. She stood and wiped away tears. "I just want to thank God for bringing me back to Bloom Hollow."

She looked down at Kirk with such love and devotion that Ben's cheeks warmed. "And I thank Him for giving me a husband who stood by my side through breast cancer and all the physical, mental, emotional and spiritual trials that went along with it."

She held her hand against her chest as she looked around the room at their church family. "I know I'm taking forever, but I have to thank God for my boys. It is by His grace that He allowed us to have children, even after conquering cancer."

As she handed the microphone back to Kent, he wrapped one arm around her shoulder in a side hug. "And conquer it, you did. God is so good." He lifted the microphone high. "Anyone else?"

Jack accepted it. "I praise God that next month I will have been an alcohol-free Christian for five years. God took me off the streets and allowed me to reunite with my family."

Several "amens" sounded from the congregation, and Maggie peeked up at Ben, her eyes widened in surprise. He nodded that Jack's words were true.

A few more people offered thanks before Pastor Kent walked back to the podium and opened his Bible. "I just want to share one Scripture tonight, and it might seem a little out of place for a Thanksgiving service. However, if you'll listen to what Jesus was saying, you'll know it fits perfectly."

The overhead screens changed, and *Matthew* 6:21 flashed on them. Pastor Kent said, "For where your treasure is, there your heart will be also."

He walked the length of the stage pointing to the congregation. "Each and every one of you has so much to be thankful for." He opened his arms wide. "Every one of us here has more than we need. Where your treasure is, your heart is."

He pointed back to the crowd. "May your treasure be Christ."

As Pastor Kent closed in prayer, Ben realized how God had worked everything out in his life to bring him back to God. If he'd gotten a job right after graduating, Ben might have continued to gamble, found himself in even more debt and possibly even ruined his reputation in the engineering world. Instead, Ben had been forced back home, where his family and church still loved him, and God wooed him back to Himself. *Thank You, Lord.*

The service closed, and they headed back to the parking lot. Maggie grabbed his arm and looked up at him. She seemed troubled, and he wished he could share some of the thanksgiving filling his heart. "I didn't know Callie had cancer," she said.

"Yeah. It was a really scary time. Both of her parents died from cancer. She and Kirk had just decided to get married when she found out she had it."

Her brows furrowed into a straight line. "And I didn't know Jack was an alcoholic."

Ben nodded. "He was gone from my sister and nieces for eight years."

"Eight years? Are you serious?" she said, her eyebrows lifting in surprise.

"Yeah. It was really hard for me to forgive him." His cheeks and neck warmed. "In fact, it's just been recently that I've begun to understand what he went through."

The need to tell Maggie about his gambling problem swelled within him, but now wasn't the time or place. He needed to tell her the truth, though, and soon. He cared about her and Pete, but they needed to build a relationship of trust.

Maggie shook her head. "You all seem so perfect."

Ben chortled. "Nobody's perfect, Maggie."

Her eyes brimmed with tears. "When Paul died, I felt like I was the only woman in the world who'd experienced such pain." She looked up at him. "He was a good man, and I loved him, and he would have loved Petey."

Ben swallowed back a mixture of sadness and jealousy, even though his mind knew he should be happy Maggie's husband had been good to her.

She continued, "And now with Aunt Jane and the house and the shop." She bit her bottom lip. "I thought I was doing the right thing by moving here to help her."

Ben touched her cheek and swiped away a tear. "I, for one, am glad you moved here."

She chuckled. "I'm glad you're glad." She exhaled a long sigh. "But so far I haven't helped much."

He wanted to refute her words, but something held him back. Her contemplative expression. Maybe the tone of her voice. But she was searching, and he needed to be quiet and allow God to work in her heart.

She motioned toward her car, and he turned and saw her aunt waving to her to come on. "I'm going to be thinking about all Pastor Kent said."

"Me, too."

As Maggie hopped in her car, Ben lifted up a quick prayer that Christ would be his treasure, the main treasure of his heart. But he wanted Maggie to be his second.

Chapter 10

Maggie finished vacuuming the guest rooms at the B and B then put the vacuum cleaner away. With Thanksgiving past, the Jacobs family no longer sold apples and pumpkins, and cooler temperatures meant people weren't bringing their kids to the activity center or petting zoo. Tammie said she wanted Maggie to keep cleaning and working in the gift shop, but Maggie knew her assistance wasn't really needed, and she wondered if her part-time employment would soon come to an end.

Walking down the stairs, she breathed in the delicious scent of cinnamon. She made her way to the kitchen and found Callie mixing applesauce and cinnamon in a bowl while Pamela flattened more of the brown substance on wax paper.

"What are you two doing?" she asked.

"Making cinnamon-applesauce ornaments," said Pamela, as she stuck a stocking-shaped cookie cutter into the concoction.

"It smells delicious," said Maggie.

"Yeah," said Callie, "and they stay that way. All you have to do is mix the cinnamon and applesauce, flatten it, cut out the shapes..."

Pamela finished, "Leave them on the cookie sheet for three or four days, and you have the best-smelling ornaments around."

"Better than any candle," said Callie.

"A lot cheaper, too," added Pamela. She nodded toward the unopened jar of applesauce. "You wanna help? Mixing bowls are in the top cabinet on the left."

"Sure." Maggie washed her hands then got out a bowl and spoon and mixed the ingredients according to the directions.

"I do this every year with children's church," said Pamela. "The kids take them home as Christmas presents to their parents." She gasped and covered her mouth with the back of her hand.

Maggie chuckled. "I won't tell Petey, and I'll still act surprised."

"So how do you like Bloom Hollow, now that you've been here a while?" asked Callie.

"I love it. It's such a beautiful place, and the people have been so nice." She stopped mixing and looked at both of them. "I really enjoy your church and your family."

"I think there's one member of our family who's especially glad you moved here." Pamela winked.

Maggie's cheeks warmed, but she continued. "I have to admit I do miss the convenience of the big city."

Callie shook her head. "Not me. I hated living in the

city. Coming back to Bloom Hollow was like coming home."

Pamela elbowed her sister-in-law. "You *were* coming home, silly. You were raised in Bloom Hollow."

Callie nodded. "You're right."

Maggie pondered Callie's words. She wasn't sure that Bloom Hollow felt that way to her. Of course, the town shouldn't, anyway. She wasn't raised here. Originally, Maggie thought she was supposed to come and help her aunt, but as each day passed, she became less sure.

"So you think you'd move back to a city?" asked Pamela.

Maggie shrugged. "I don't know. I thought I had my life all planned out. All I've ever wanted to be was a wife and mom, but then Paul died."

"I'm sorry," said Callie. "How long has it been?"

"Four years. I was still pregnant with Petey." She flattened her mixture on wax paper. "I miss him, of course, but I'm ready to move on with life. I just don't know how." She picked up a star cookie cutter. "I still just want to be a wife and mom, so where does that leave me?"

Pamela took a toothpick and stuck holes in the top of each of her ornaments. "It is tricky when plans don't work out the way you think. I thought Jack would stay with me forever, then he was gone. Then I thought I'd get my accounting degree and provide for me and the girls. Then Jack came back. Now I'm about to graduate, and I'm not sure if I'm going to go for an accounting job or just keep working on the family farm."

Callie said, "Plus you have that great new house."

Pamela sighed. "I love my new house." She nudged Maggie's arm. "Let's finish up here then we'll walk over and take a tour."

"Okay," said Maggie.

Callie finished her ornaments then washed her hands. "Back to the topic of change. That's why we have to stay close to God. Life is always changing. Never exactly what we expected or planned for."

Maggie pressed the toothpick holes in her ornaments then threw away the empty jars of applesauce and cinnamon. "Yeah, I just wish He'd tell me straight out what I need to do."

Callie chuckled. "Wouldn't we all. Don't worry. He'll show you."

Once they'd cleaned the kitchen, they walked toward Pamela's finished home. Ben stepped out of the cabin. She grinned, knowing he was glad to have his own space. "Hey. Where you all going?"

"Taking Maggie to show off my house," said Pamela.

"Can I talk to her for a minute?" He looked at Pamela and Callie then turned to Maggie and pointed at her. "Talk to you? For just a minute?"

"Sure." Pamela and Callie winked at each other.

Maggie's heartbeat raced, partially from excitement and partly from embarrassment. She looked at him and realized he'd shoved both fists in his front jeans pockets.

He cleared his throat. "With Christmas in a couple weeks, I wondered if I could take you shopping. For Pete."

Maggie nodded. "That would be great."

"Then maybe we could go to dinner."

"As a date?"

"Yeah."

Maggie grinned. "Our last date didn't exactly work out as planned."

"Maybe this time it will."

"I'd like that. Now I'd better catch up with Callie and Pamela."

"You're going to get the third degree. They're going to want to know everything we said."

"Oh, I know."

Concern enveloped his expression, and he touched her elbow. "Wait a minute. What have they said already?"

Maggie laughed. "Nothing much." She walked away then looked back and winked. She was full-fledged flirting with him. And it felt great.

Ben wrapped his hand around Maggie's and tried to turn her toward the car. "I assure you, Pete is going to have a great time."

Maggie stammered, "It's…just…"

Callie waved at them. "Go on. He's going to do great. He's already playing with the boys. Have fun."

Maggie opened her mouth then snapped her lips closed. Ben squeezed her hand. "Let's go shop."

She grinned at him as he opened the car door for her. "Do you really like to shop, or was this your way to make sure we were alone?"

"Truth?"

"Yes."

"I hate to shop."

Maggie swatted his arm, and Ben grabbed his biceps and feigned injury. "Give a guy a break. I wanted to spend some time with you."

She twisted in the seat. "I guess I have to admit I think it's kind of sweet that you'd suffer through a day of shopping with me."

He pumped his fist in the air. "Yes. Already on her good side."

"You're silly."

"Sometimes. So where are we going first?"

"Toy store. I don't have a lot of money to spend, but

I have to buy some toy horses, since someone got him hooked on the animal."

Ben lifted his hands in surrender. "Not my fault he's a smart kid."

Once inside the toy store, Ben felt like a kid again. Everywhere they turned he spotted some kind of gadget he wanted to play with Pete. But, like Maggie, he had a limited budget, and he wanted to buy her something, as well.

Maggie picked up a country farm set. The box said the toy was for ages five to ten, but it was perfect for Pete. It had a barn, a couple of horses, a couple of people and lots of things to set up around the barn. Bushes, trough, shovel. Ben pointed to the age. "I don't think he's too young for it. Looks perfect to me."

"I think so, too. But seventy dollars is more than I'd planned to spend."

Ben raised his brows. He hadn't noticed the price. That was a lot of money for one toy. "Can I look at it?"

The set included trees and a fence. Pete could even open up the barn and set up the stables and the hayloft. When Ben was a kid, he'd have spent hours playing with this toy. "Why don't you let me get it for him?"

Maggie frowned. "What? No way."

"I was gonna get him something, anyway."

Maggie stared at the box while Ben stuck it in the cart. "Come on. What else are we looking at?" He rubbed his belly. "I'm getting hungry."

"I want to look at blocks."

"You know the expense is gonna really get ugly when the boy is old enough for electronics."

Maggie lifted her hand. "I don't even want to think about it."

Ben followed her around the store, remembering why he hated to go shopping with his mother. For every item

Maggie looked at, she'd pick up two almost identical toys, read the labels, compare the pictures and the prices, decide on one then change her mind and select the other. By the time she'd said she was finished, Ben thought he would pull his hair out. Or maybe even hers. With purchases bought and tucked away in the trunk, he drove to the steakhouse.

Since the dinner crowd had long since finished eating, and his stomach could feel it, they were seated right away. He didn't have to look at the menu. He ordered the same dinner each time he came.

Maggie took a sip of her soft drink then grinned. "You did good, Ben."

"What do you mean?"

"You didn't complain one time."

"I thought my stomach was eating itself."

Maggie laughed, and Ben smiled back at her. He'd had a great time. If she learned to love him half as much as she loved her son, he wouldn't know what to do with all her attention. He cared about her. A lot. Like in a forever and ever kind of way. He'd have thought he'd have been scared by the feelings, but he wasn't. Every fiber in him wanted to be there for Maggie, do whatever she needed, give her whatever she wanted. He loved her.

Which was why he needed to tell her about the gambling. Come clean about why his student loans were more than they should have been. It was also why he prayed God would provide him a job. Soon.

The waitress arrived with their orders, and she reached for his hands. He tried to focus on praying, and yet part of his mind relished the soft feel of her skin. She started talking about Christmas plans and church activities and a lunch date she and Pamela and Callie had planned. He couldn't find a time that seemed right to tell her about his past.

Kirk had driven Pete home when her aunt Jane got back from her dinner with friends, so Ben drove Maggie to her house. She unlocked the consignment shop, and they stashed her presents in a closet in the back room.

When they stepped onto the store's porch, Maggie's hair glistened in the full moon's light. The cool December air had kissed her nose and cheeks from the trip to and from the car. She looked up at him, and Ben felt as though he was drowning in her deep blue eyes.

His gaze lowered to her lips then back up to her eyes. She parted her lips just slightly, and Ben lifted her chin with his thumb. Lowering his head, he brushed his lips against hers in the slightest whisper of a kiss.

He straightened his shoulders and caressed her cheek with his fingertip. "I had a good time, Maggie."

"Me, too."

"We need to do it again sometime. Soon."

"I agree."

He watched as she walked across the yard to her house. She waved once more before she stepped inside and closed the door behind her. Yes, they'd have to share another date. Very soon.

Chapter 11

Maggie had thought about Ben's kiss long into the night. She'd wanted more than just a brush of his lips, and yet she appreciated that he wasn't trying to move too fast. She checked the closet door where they'd hidden the presents last night, then she pulled down the puzzles Petey liked from the bookshelf.

"Fank you, Mommy."

She tousled his hair. "You're welcome, Petey."

He shook his head and pointed to his chest. "Pete."

She frowned. "You don't want Mommy to call you Petey anymore?"

He shook his head with more emphasis, and Maggie blinked back the threat of tears. Her baby had already grown up so much. Now he didn't want her to call him by his nickname. Before she knew it, she'd be escorting him to kindergarten, buying him a shaving kit, teaching him to drive, sending him to college. *Way to be overly dramatic. The child just turned four.* Still, the thought of her baby boy growing up sent flashes of pain through her heart.

She kissed the top of his head. "Okay, big boy. Pete. Mommy's going to check on the front of the store."

The door opened and the bell rang. Maggie sucked in her breath when Carl Pearson walked in. "Hello, Carl. How can I help you?"

He pointed toward the house. "Jane told me I could walk through the house today."

Maggie scratched her forehead, fearing that was exactly what he'd say. "She must have forgotten to tell me, and she's not here right now. I don't have anyone to watch the store."

Carl's expression dropped. "I took off work this afternoon to stop by."

Maggie felt bad for the guy. She'd asked Aunt Jane several times when Carl planned to come back, and she kept telling Maggie not to worry, that she'd take care of it. Her aunt's mind seemed to be clear as crystal when she wanted to remember something but would fog over whenever Maggie tried to discuss finances or anything Aunt Jane wasn't interested in or didn't want to discuss.

Maggie chewed on the inside of her cheek as she glanced at the insurance broker. She wouldn't be surprised if her aunt was matchmaking again. Especially since Maggie told her in plain terms that she was not interested in their next-door neighbor.

She took a sheet of paper out from beside the register and wrote a quick note that said she'd be right back. Taping it to the door, she then pointed to the back. "Let me get Petey. I mean, my son, Pete, and I'll take you on a quick tour." She lifted her eyebrows. "But I'm warning you. The place was a mess when I left it this morning."

He chuckled. "That's quite all right. I'm most interested in the structure and layout."

The three walked to the house and she opened the door. Just as she remembered, breakfast dishes sat on TV trays in the living room. Dirty clothes were piled in front of the washing machine. She tried to push back her embarrassment at the disaster in the room she shared with Pete. Trying to think positively, she wondered if the mess would keep Carl from wanting to purchase the house and shop.

Once he'd tested the sinks, toilets, light switches and the heating and air-conditioning unit, she locked up the house and they walked back to the consignment shop.

"Both buildings are in terrific shape," said Carl. "They're older, so I'm sure they require a bit more loving care, but overall, they look great."

Maggie forced herself to smile at his praise. The words didn't sound like those of a man who planned to run for the hills from their excess laundry buildup. She decided to try a different approach. Make him feel guilty. "Yes. Pete and I really like it. We just moved here a few months ago to help Aunt Jane keep the store running."

He grimaced. "Yes, Jane told me. But she said the business hasn't really picked up."

Maggie's hope that he'd feel guilty deflated. "No. It hasn't." Not wanting to talk about any of this anymore, Maggie said, "I'll tell Aunt Jane you came by today."

"I'd appreciate it." He shoved one hand into his pants pocket. "I…uh…left a business card the last time I was here. Did you see it?"

Maggie's heart pounded in her chest. She did not want this man to ask her out on a date. He seemed like a nice guy, but if she was going to fall for anyone, Ben was her pick. And if her aunt sold the house and shop, Maggie might need to rethink falling for him, because she might have to move to the other side of Tennessee to live with her mother.

The thought sent a slice of pain through Maggie's body. She didn't want to move away from her new church family or from the Jacobses.

"I did see the card."

"Oh." His gaze darted from her to the room then back to her.

Come on, Carl. Take the hint. Don't ask me out.

He continued, "I was wondering if you'd like to have coffee sometime. Maybe get a bite to eat."

Maggie clasped her hands. "Well, I have Pete, and it's sometimes difficult to find someone to watch him."

He leaned closer to her. "I'm sure your aunt wouldn't mind."

Wrong answer, buddy. Maggie would only consider a man who knew that she and Pete were a two-for-one package, and as such, he'd have to be willing to take the four-year-old on a date when necessary.

"The truth is I'm kind of seeing someone."

"Really?"

Carl's expression betrayed complete surprise, and Maggie felt the hackles rise on the back of her neck. Was she not cute enough? Or was having a son so much of a burden that most guys wouldn't want to give her the time of day? If this dude didn't watch it, she was going to pounce on him.

She cocked her head. "Yes. Believe it or not."

He must have figured out how rude he'd sounded, because he pulled his hand out of his pocket and straightened his shoulders. "Well, I'd best be going, then. Please be sure to tell Jane I saw the house."

Maggie waved. "I will."

Still feeling insulted, Maggie rummaged through the clothes racks to be sure the sizes were in correct order. She checked the tags on the miscellaneous items on the shelves then checked on Pete.

What a day. First, her son told her he was too old for the name she'd called him since birth. Then Carl took a tour of her home—that she had no desire to sell—and then he'd acted shocked that someone would actually want to date her. She felt like a worn doormat unfit for salvage.

Okay, she was being too sensitive. But she didn't want her boy to become so independent, and she didn't want Aunt Jane to sell the house. She thought of Callie's comment that life was always changing, that we had to trust God. She blew out a breath. *God, I want to trust You, but I feel like something's off between me and You. Am I doing something wrong? Show me.*

Ben parked in front of Jane's Treasures. He'd thought about his and Maggie's date throughout the night, relished the memory of their brief kiss. He'd driven himself crazy thinking about her while tending the farm. After lunch, he couldn't stand it any longer. He had to see her again.

He saw her through the oversize store window. She stood behind the counter talking with a customer. Her blond hair flowed freely down her shoulders and back. With each nod of her head, he envisioned her sky-blue eyes twinkling and a smile lifting her lips.

The customer, a man, leaned forward, and Ben's heart pounded against his chest. Heat rushed up and down his neck, through his arms and he balled his fists. The fellow was doing a little more than buying clothes or knickknacks. He appeared to be flirting with Maggie. His Maggie. And Ben didn't like it one bit.

He glanced at the dark green Honda parked beside his truck. He didn't recognize the vehicle. Squinting to try to get a better view of the customer, he didn't recognize the man, either.

Gripping the steering wheel with both hands, he moved his fists forward and exhaled a deep breath. Wouldn't do for him to get out and try to talk to her right now. If he did he might say or do something to the fellow that Ben might later regret.

He counted to ten. Twice. If the man didn't hurry up and leave, Ben would have to go inside. *Come on out, man. You and I both don't want that to happen.*

After counting to ten one more time, the front door opened and the thin, dark-haired guy walked out. Pencil pusher. No doubt about it. Ben held back a chuckle. Once he landed an electrical engineering position, he'd be pushing a pencil part of the time, as well.

He got out of the truck and nodded to Desk Job Dude. The man returned the nod, and Ben's heart lightened that the guy didn't look overly happy. Walking into the store, he grinned at Maggie. "Hey. How's my favorite consignment store lady?"

Pete heard him, raced to the front and wrapped his arms around Ben's leg. "Mr. Ben."

Ben lowered his hand with his palm up, and Pete gave him a high five. "I just swung by to see if your mom would let you take a break from work."

Pete giggled. "I'm not working, Mr. Ben."

Ben winked. "Well, then, maybe you'd like to go with me to get an ice cream."

Pete jumped up and down. "Can I, Mommy? Can I?"

"Sure." Maggie motioned to the back room. "Get your coat."

While Pete raced out of the room, Ben leaned on the counter and nodded toward the window. "Customer?"

She shook her head and dropped her shoulders. "No. He came to look at the house."

"What?"

"Aunt Jane's still talking about selling the house and the shop. You know we're barely making ends meet."

Ben chewed the inside of his lip. He knew things were tight. The consignment store hadn't had much business in years. Ever, that he could remember. But he didn't know they were actually showing the house and business. Her aunt planned to move halfway across the state with Maggie's mom, and he had no idea what Maggie planned. *God, she can't move.* "Was he interested in making an offer?"

She shrugged. "I couldn't tell for sure."

"He seemed interested in *you*." The moment the words slipped from his lips, Ben wished he could bite them back. He balled his fists again. This time wishing he could deck himself.

Maggie cocked her head and grinned. "You thought so, huh?"

Ben clamped his lips together, refusing to answer the question.

She leaned forward and rested her elbows on the counter then batted her eyes. "Would that have bothered you if he was?"

Ben yelled, "Pete, you find your coat yet?"

Maggie laughed as she stood back up. "I'm going to take that as a yes, and as a compliment."

Ben glanced back at her, noting her eyes still twinkled

with mischief. "You better take that cute look off your face, or I'm going to have to kiss it off."

She lifted her lips into a smile that would rival the Cheshire cat from *Alice in Wonderland.* "We'll see."

He liked where this relationship seemed to be heading. A lot. Whatever it took, he couldn't let her and Pete move away. Unless it was with him.

Pete ran from the back room. "I'm ready, Mr. Ben."

The boy's coat wasn't zipped, and one of his shoes was untied. Bending down, Ben fixed Pete's clothes. When he stood up, Maggie smiled at him with such sweetness she'd have been able to ask for anything and he would have done it for her.

He tapped Pete's hat. "All right, big guy. Let's go."

Pete waved. "Bye, Mommy."

She lifted both palms in the air. "What? No hug or kiss?"

Pete ran around the counter and wrapped both arms around her legs. She kissed his forehead then patted his back. "Be good for Mr. Ben."

"I will."

Once outside, Ben took the child's booster seat from Maggie's car and secured it onto his backseat. With Pete buckled in, he saw Maggie looking out the window. She smiled, and her whole face lit up. He cared about her. More than he thought possible, having known her for such a short time.

He pulled out of the parking space. Looking in the rearview mirror, he said, "Pete, after ice cream, what do you say we go buy your mommy a Christmas present?"

"Okay. She likes to color pictures." He tapped his finger against his cheek. A gesture Ben had seen Maggie do. "And she likes to read books. Specially, Dr. Seuss."

Ben held back a chuckle. Maggie's present from Pete might be interesting.

Chapter 12

Maggie covered her face with both hands. She couldn't pay the bills and buy groceries. It was one or the other. Through Christmas and New Year's, she'd been glad they hadn't heard from Carl Pearson with an offer on the house and store. Now she didn't know what they would do to keep from going under.

The consignment store had a bit of business from Thanksgiving to Christmas, enough that she bought a few presents for Pete and made a few items for her mom, sister and Aunt Jane. Her cheeks warmed again when she thought about Ben giving her a spa package from one of the nicer department stores in the mall, as well as a certificate to get her hair cut and her nails done. She'd teased that he must think she looked a mess but she knew he was just offering her a bit of pampering. How many times had he told her she worked too hard?

She plopped the electric bill onto the table. Obviously, not hard enough.

"What's the matter, dear?" Aunt Jane stood beside her, squinting at the computer screen. Her bright pink lipstick clashed with the orange-and-red sweater her aunt wore. She held a cup between both swollen hands, lifted it to her lips and took a sip, leaving a bright pink stain around the rim.

Maggie sighed. "Nothing. It'll work out."

"Bills again, huh?"

Maggie stared at the screen, wishing just once she'd see black instead of red. "I don't know what to do."

"It's time to sell, Maggie. I know you've put up a good fight."

She glanced up. The determined set in Aunt Jane's jaw broke Maggie's heart. Her aunt had lived her entire life in this house. The only real job the woman had had was running the consignment store. Maggie couldn't take this away from her. Somehow she had to make it work. Had to come up with additional regular income. She wished she knew more about marketing. Getting people to want to visit the shop.

Unable to look her aunt in the eye, she closed the laptop and stood. "I'll figure something out."

"Maggie."

"Aunt Jane, I will. I promise."

She walked into her bedroom and picked up her cell phone from the dresser. After pushing her mom's name, she tapped her fingers on the wood while she waited for Mom to pick up.

"Hello."

"Mom, I need help.... I don't know what to do."

Maggie bit her bottom lip and blinked back tears. Her chest swelled with emotion. She hadn't realized how deep-down fatigued she'd felt. Probably for far too long. Years, even.

"Maggie, what's the matter?"

"I can't do it, Mom. I'm working every chance I can, but the numbers won't match up." Her voice caught in the back of her throat, and she swallowed and swiped at her eyes with her free hand.

"Maggie, it's time to let the place go. Even Aunt Jane thinks so. You heard her while you all were here over the holidays."

Christmas at her mom's house had been wonderful. More food than four women and one little boy could eat. Turkey and ham, mashed potatoes and sweet potato casserole, corn pudding and green beans, rolls and pumpkin pie. They'd sat around the table and talked, laughed and played games. Pete had gotten enough clothes and toys from his aunt and grandma that she wouldn't have to buy him anything for a year, or until he outgrew them all. Everything had been perfect. Except Aunt Jane's insistence that they sell the house and shop and she move in with her niece, Maggie's mom.

"Mom, deep down, you know Aunt Jane doesn't want to move."

Her mom clicked her tongue. "No, Maggie. I think she does."

"You don't see her here. The expression on her face when we talk about it. The set in her jaw. It's her way of trying not to be emotional about moving."

"Are you sure you're not reading her wrong? That place has been too much for her to handle for quite some time."

"If I could just figure a way to increase sales at the shop."

"Maggie."

"Mom, I have to keep trying." She raked her hand through her hair. "Look, I'd better go. I'll call you later. Love you."

A long sigh sounded over the phone then her mom said, "I love you, too."

Maggie placed the phone on the dresser then flopped onto the bed. She closed her eyes, thankful she didn't have to worry about what Pete was up to since he'd fallen asleep on the couch. *God, I don't know what to do.*

Frustration swelled within her. No matter how many times she called out to God about their money situation, He seemed quiet. No answers. No peace settling in her heart.

She thought of the sermon several weeks back when Pastor Kent talked about trusting God with all your heart, believing that He'd work everything out. Something like that. She trusted God. At least, she was trying to.

He'd also said to look at what was happening around you, that God spoke to His children through the Bible, but He also used circumstances and other people. But that didn't make sense to Maggie. Her mom was wrong about this, and Aunt Jane didn't *really* want to sell. Aunt Jane just didn't know how to fix the problem.

Maggie lifted her arms, intertwined her fingers and placed her hands under her head. *I don't know how to fix it, either.*

Releasing a long, slow breath, she tried to erase the worry from her mind. If only for a few minutes. Pete was asleep. A power nap might do her some good, as well.

A drip sounded from across the hall. Maggie rolled over to her side, cupping her hands under her cheek.

Another plop.

She moved her shoulder into a more comfortable position.

Plop again.

You've got to be kidding me. She jumped out of the bed and stomped to the bathroom. She turned on the faucet and let the water flow then shut it off. A plop dropped into the sink. *Great. Now the faucet needs to be fixed.*

A full week had passed since Ben last saw Maggie and Pete. Ten days to be exact. He'd been busy enough. A few engineering jobs opened up in Knoxville. He sent the companies his résumé, researched the firms and sent emails to a few heavy hitters at each place. Even called his references to let them know they might be hearing from someone soon. But when Christmas passed and New Year's arrived, getting a kiss from his nieces and Mom just wasn't the same as sharing one with Maggie.

He'd seen her and Pete at church on Sunday, and Maggie would be coming to the farm to clean the B and B in a couple of days, but he couldn't wait that long. He hopped out of his dad's truck, walked up the steps and knocked on the door. Her aunt Jane opened it. He nodded. "Hey."

She smiled, but the smile didn't fully reach her eyes. She opened the door wider. "Come on in, Ben."

He obliged. "Did you have a nice Christmas and New Year's?"

Her expression softened, if only a bit. "Yes. We had a lovely time at my niece's home. Such a lovely house. Open floor plan with a kitchen any woman would dream of. And the bedrooms are just wonderful."

Maggie walked into the room. Bags hung beneath her eyes, but the smile she offered was warm and genuine. His heartbeat sped up. She pointed to the couch and whispered, "I thought I heard you."

He placed his finger over his lips. "Didn't see the little guy sleeping there when I walked in."

"If the two of you will excuse me," said Aunt Jane, "I'm going to head back to the dining room to finish my project."

She left, and Ben said, "It amazes me that she paints those wooden figurines like she does."

"Those arthritic hands don't stop Aunt Jane. She's the feistiest woman I know," said Maggie.

He still stood several feet away from her. Everything in him wanted to close the distance and wrap his arms around her. "So how was Christmas?"

"Wonderful. How about yours?"

"Noisy as always. But a lot of fun." He winked. "I missed you on New Year's."

She covered her mouth to stifle a laugh. "You're determined to get another kiss, aren't you?"

He shrugged. "I wouldn't mind." He lifted his hands. "I mean, I wouldn't put up a fight or anything."

She shook her head. "Before we think about any of that, I need a favor." She furrowed her brows.

"Anything. What do you need?"

She pointed down the hall. "The bathroom faucet is dripping."

"I'll take a look."

He followed her down the hall and to the small bathroom. The drip was no problem at all. Just a loose ring. She fetched him a wrench, and he tightened it up. "All done."

She breathed a sigh of relief. "I'm so glad it was an easy fix."

He lifted one eyebrow. "I'm sorry, ma'am, but a man should still be paid for his efforts."

Maggie cocked her head and placed her hands on her hips. "Really."

Ben crossed his arms in front of his chest. He nodded

toward the sink. "I imagine if you'd called a plumber he'd have charged you fifty bucks or more just to show up."

"You're most likely right, so what do you suggest?"

He twisted his mouth to the side. "How 'bout a hug for now?"

Opening his arms wide, he was surprised that she quickly obliged, welcoming his embrace and wrapping her arms around him. Her hair smelled like cinnamon and vanilla, and he breathed his fill. "I missed you."

"I missed you, too."

"Mommy," Pete hollered then walked down the hall, wiping his eyes. "I took a nap." He looked up and noticed Ben. "Mr. Ben."

"Hey, buddy. I came to see if you and your mommy wanted to go with me to get a hamburger."

"Yeah." Pete clapped his hands.

Maggie squinted at him. "Have you noticed you always ask Pete instead of me?"

Heat rushed to Ben's face. "It's terrible of me, I know." He leaned down and whispered in her ear. "But then you can't say no."

He stood to his full height, and Maggie punched his arm. "Ben Jacobs."

Lifting his hands in surrender, he chuckled. "Guilty as charged."

"You wanna see my new toys 'fore we go?" asked Pete.

"Sure."

Maggie pointed to the dining room. "I'll ask Aunt Jane if she wants us to pick up anything for her."

Ben oohed and aahed after each toy, and even tried his hand at a few of the action figures. His phone rang. Ben recognized the number as one of the firms where he'd sent his résumé.

With excitement filling his chest, he lifted his finger to Pete and said, "I'll be right back."

He stepped into the hall, cleared his throat and answered the phone. "Ben Jacobs."

"Hello, Mr. Jacobs," a nasally female voice responded. "I'm calling from PGM Associates about the engineer opening."

"Yes, ma'am."

"We'd like to set up an interview. Would you be available tomorrow morning at ten-thirty?"

Adrenaline raced through his veins. *God, let this be it. The job I've been waiting for.* "Yes, ma'am. That won't be a problem."

"All right. We will see you then."

"Thank you. I'm looking forward to it."

He ended the call then pumped his fist in the air. He felt good about this. Tonight he'd go home and look over their website again. Make a few calls to see what some of his friends knew about the company. He'd step into that office tomorrow and knock their socks off. Excitement bubbled up inside him, and he pumped his fist again. "All right! Game on!"

Aunt Jane stood at the end of the hallway. She pursed her lips and narrowed her gaze.

Ben didn't know what she'd be upset about, but nothing could bring him down tonight. Then he heard a choking sound from Pete's bedroom. The little guy raced past him to the bathroom. Just inside the door, he vomited.

Maggie rushed from the other room and moved him into the bathroom. "I think we're going to have to take a rain check."

"Do you need some help?"

She swatted her hand. "No. I'm a pro at this. I'll see you in a couple days."

Ben hesitated until her aunt stood beside him. She stared at him, but he couldn't read her expression. "We'll be fine," she muttered.

Taking the hint, he made his way to the door. "Call me if you need anything."

Her aunt nodded, but by the look on her face, he'd be the last person they'd call.

Chapter 13

Maggie helped Pete out of his soiled shirt. He started to whimper, and she patted his bare back. "It's okay, honey."

"It's gross," he cried.

His face was still pale, and his lip quivered. She stood him beside the toilet then grabbed paper towels and cleaning supplies from the linen closet.

Aunt Jane stood in the door. "How can I help?"

"I'm fine. I'll help Pete if you'll heat up some soup or something for dinner."

Pete shook his head. "Mommy, I still don't feel good."

"I know, sweetie." She brushed his hair away from his eyes, checking to see if he felt warm. He didn't seem to have a fever.

He stood beside her, his body trembling, while she worked quickly to clean up the mess on the floor. "You are such a big boy for running to the bathroom."

He nodded, but she could tell he would be sick again

very soon. She finished cleaning just in time. Once he'd stopped, she helped him rinse out his mouth then sat on the edge of the tub and held him in her lap. "Do you feel better?"

"A little."

She noticed his color had improved this time so she started the bath water. "You wanna take a bath?"

He nodded again. "I feel gross."

Smiling at her son, she kissed the top of his head. She didn't know many boys who hated to get dirty, but her son was one of them. He still didn't feel warm, and she hoped something had simply upset his stomach and that he wasn't getting a bug of some kind.

Once the tub was filled, she washed his hair and body, making sure no traces of vomit remained. By the time he'd gotten into his pajamas and brushed his teeth, Pete seemed to be feeling better. Even asked for food.

"Tell you what," Maggie said. "I'll let you eat some crackers and drink clear pop, okay?"

Pete nodded, and she spread a blanket on the couch and put the snack on a TV tray. He hopped onto the couch and smiled. "Fanks, Mommy."

"I don't want you to bounce around. I'll turn on a television show, but I want you to rest."

He popped a cracker into his mouth like he hadn't just spent the past hour in the bathroom. "Okay, Mommy."

Maggie's stomach rumbled, partly from cleaning up vomit and partly from hunger. Dinnertime had passed two hours ago. She walked into the kitchen. Aunt Jane had two bowls of chicken noodle soup on the table. She pointed across from her. "It's still warm. Sit and eat."

Maggie plopped into the chair. "Thanks. I'm starving and queasy all at the same time."

"We need to talk."

Maggie furrowed her brows at her aunt's firm tone. Surely she didn't want to argue about selling the house and shop right now. "Okay. Go ahead."

"I know you like Ben Jacobs."

Maggie's cheeks warmed, and she shifted in the chair. "Now, Aunt Jane, I've never said anything about—"

"I know you've never said it, but I'm not blind."

Maggie sat up straighter. Her aunt didn't have a right to dictate who she could or could not like. She respected Aunt Jane, but unless she gave her a valid reason to not like Ben, then their relationship wasn't her business.

"I'd decided not to tell you this because Tammie said he had changed. At least, she and Mike prayed he'd changed."

Maggie took a bite of the soup. Whatever it was couldn't be that bad. Ben was wonderful. She was beginning to feel that God was allowing her a second chance at true love. "Okay. What is it?"

Aunt Jane stared at her for a moment. She rubbed swollen hands together then pressed them against the edge of the table.

Maggie wiped her mouth with a paper towel. "Aunt Jane, Ben has been a complete gentleman with me. He helps in any way he can. He adores Pete. And I just don't understand why you don't—"

"He has a gambling problem. A poker problem, to be exact."

Maggie put the spoon down and gawked at her aunt. Memories of her childhood smashed against her mind. Dad coming home late. Canceled family vacations. Dance lessons stopped. Repossession of the van. Her mom struggling to make ends meet when Dad finally left for good. "What?"

Aunt Jane reached across the table and placed her hand

on Maggie's. "I wouldn't have told you. I've been praying to let it go. To give the guy a chance. The way he treated you and Pete, I thought he must have stopped. But…"

Maggie furrowed her brows. "But what?"

Aunt Jane sighed and patted her chest. "My heart just breaks for Tammie and Mike. They tried so hard to raise those kids for the Lord. And yet each one of them has faced so many trials." Her aunt clicked her tongue. "The Good Book tells us we'll face trials of every kind…"

"Aunt Jane," Maggie interrupted her. "What happened to make you decide to tell me?"

"Today when Pete showed him his new toys I heard Ben talking in the hall. He was making plans to go to a game."

Maggie's mind darted with a million thoughts. She just couldn't believe it. Her aunt had to be mistaken. A gambling problem just didn't make sense. Ben showed no signs of an addiction. He was prompt, responsible. Nothing like her father. "Maybe…maybe the plans were for something else."

"His last words were 'game on.'"

Bile rose in Maggie's throat. She covered her mouth with her hand.

"Maggie, I'm so sorry."

Tears filled her eyes, and Maggie swiped them away. How could she have been so foolish? How could she not have seen? Her mother had told them repeatedly she'd never seen their father's addiction coming. Then they were drowning in financial ruin.

"Mommy!" Pete's squeal sounded from the living room, followed by a hacking sound.

Maggie groaned as she ran into the living room. Pete had thrown up all over himself and the blanket. "Pete,

why didn't you go to the bathroom? You had to have
known you were about to get sick again," she barked.

With his arms held out at his sides, tears spilled down
his cheeks. "I don't know, Mommy."

Feeling like the lousiest mother in the world, she
helped him out of his clothes. "I'm sorry, Pete. Mommy
shouldn't have fussed at you. It's not your fault you're
sick."

"I sorry, Mommy," he cried.

Tears filled her eyes again. This time she allowed them
to fall. "No, honey. Mommy was wrong to snap at you.
Come on. We'll get cleaned up again."

And we'll clean up more than just the vomit. She would
not risk her son's future on a man with a gambling problem. She moved to Bloom Hollow to do a job. Help her
aunt. And start fresh with her son. She was determined
to rid herself of anything that could jeopardize those ob-
jectives. And now that included Ben Jacobs.

Life couldn't be any better for Ben Jacobs. *Thank You,
God, for this interview. It's the one. The job You've prepared for me. I can feel it in my bones.*

He added a prayer that Pete would feel better soon, and
that Maggie and Jane wouldn't contract whatever bug he
had. When he walked into the house, he was surprised
to see most of the family there. Mom. Dad. Kirk. Jack,
Pamela and the girls. "What's the special occasion?"

Pamela shrugged. "No special occasion. Mom just
called and asked if we wanted to come over to watch a
movie and eat popcorn."

Jack scratched the stubble on his chin. "Since the drive
wasn't too far."

Pamela laughed and shoved his arm.

"Dad, we just had to walk here," said Emmy.

Emma rolled her eyes. "No duh. Dad was kidding."

"Oh," said Emmy.

"Where're the boys?" asked Ben.

Kirk tilted his head. "Do you really think those two would make it through a movie?"

"No, but…"

Kirk interrupted. "They were already heading to bed. Callie just decided to stay with them and finish some laundry."

Mom smiled and waved her hand at him. "You kind of have a glow about you."

"We'll have no glows in this house," his dad piped up.

"Not until he's married, anyway," teased Kirk.

Ben narrowed his gaze. "You two are just a barrel of laughs." He clasped his hands and rubbed them together. "But I do have good news."

His dad sat up. "Terrific. Let's hear it."

"I got a job interview."

"Great."

"Terrific."

"That's wonderful news," said his mom. "Who with?"

He shared about the company with his family and the interview the following day. "I'm going to head over to the cabin now to get my suit ready and to check out their website again."

"Honey, I'm so happy. I'll be praying for you," said Mom.

"Why not pray right now?" responded Dad.

Pamela stood and held out her hands. "That sounds like a great idea."

The rest of the family got into a circle and grabbed hands. A few months ago Ben would have been bothered by this, felt like their petitions were in vain, but God had brought him a long way in his faith since he'd returned to Bloom Hollow.

"Dear Father," his dad's voice boomed through the room. "We praise You for Ben and the work You've done in his life. We thank You that he is once again seeking Your will."

A quiet "amen" slipped from his mother's and Pamela's lips. Ben squeezed his sister's hand to let her know how much he appreciated her belief in him.

"Go before him at this interview tomorrow. Give him the right words to say. And, Lord, we ask that if this is not the right job for him that he will not get it."

Ben squirmed at his father's prayer. This was the right job. He just knew it.

"Regardless, may he leave that place knowing You were there with him. In Your name we pray. Amen."

His mom and then Pamela wrapped him in a hug. Dad patted his back. "I'm proud of you, son. God's working in your life."

Ben nodded. His dad's words were true. Renewed faith. Maggie and Pete. And now a job interview.

"You sure you don't want to stay and watch the movie with us?" asked Mom.

Ben shook his head. "I want to be prepared for the morning."

"That's my boy," said Dad.

He started toward the door then turned. "I do have a question."

They all looked up at him, and Ben wished he'd just called Mom and asked her one-on-one. Oh well, they all figured he liked her, anyway. "Mom, what do you think about asking Maggie, Pete and Jane to dinner?"

Her eyes twinkled as Pamela, Kirk and Jack started saying, "Ohhhhh."

"I think Maggie's pretty," said Emma.

"And Pete is just adorable," added Emmy.

"Sounds like a good idea to me, Ben. She's coming to clean tomorrow. I'll ask her then," said Mom.

"Don't tell her about the interview. I want to do that."

"Okay."

He waved then headed to the cabin. After pulling out his navy blue suit, he decided on a red tie with a diagonal stripe pattern. He found his black dress shoes in the back of the closet and shined the toes. Then he ironed a white button-down shirt. Using the clippers, he trimmed his sideburns and took great care to be sure the hair at the base of his head formed a straight line above his neck. And no scraggly hairs beneath it.

Having done the best he could with his appearance, he settled at the table and turned on the laptop. He scoured the company's website once again, making notes of names and positions, mission statements and goals. Calling his references to let them know he had an interview scheduled, he was thrilled to discover the company had already contacted them. *God, that means they're interested.*

Ben stood, touched his palms together then pressed his pointer fingers against his lips. "I have no idea how I'm going to sleep tonight."

He walked into the bedroom and pulled down the covers. Spying his Bible and devotional on the nightstand, he slid into bed and picked them up. He read the daily devotion then flipped to the concordance in the Bible. Looking up the word *peace,* he devoured verse after verse, allowing his fears to abate.

As fatigue finally started to settle in, he grabbed his cell phone off the nightstand and texted Maggie. He didn't tell her about the interview. Not yet. Just wanted to let her know he was there if they needed anything. After a last prayer that they would have a good night and that Pete would feel better, peace finally washed over him. Tomorrow was a new day. A good one. Then he went to sleep dreaming of a woman, a boy and a job.

Chapter 14

Pete got sick one more time in the night. Not that it really mattered. His sickness didn't interrupt her sleep, as she hadn't been able to close her eyes longer than five minutes after what Aunt Jane had shared about Ben.

Satisfied that Pete's stomach had settled enough to leave him with her aunt, Maggie staggered to the car the next morning and made her way to the Jacobs Family Farm to clean the B and B. Tired or not, devastated or not, she couldn't call Tammie and feign sickness. They really needed the money.

She walked into the yellow guest room. The room was by far her favorite. Facing the front of the home, a small nook had been built around the window. White blinds framed with yellow-flowered drapes hung above a white bench in the small area. The bench opened and inside Tammie stored several classic novels, *Anne of Green Gables*, *Little Women*, *Pride and Prejudice* and many more.

The nook was Maggie's favorite part of the room. A place she'd often envisioned nestling up with several pillows and one of the classics. The first thing the guests would notice was the queen-size bed adorned in a pure white quilt with small yellow roses stitched into the center of each square. A white canopy flowed above the bed with lace and yellow ribbon hanging from the hem.

Pure feminine beauty. That's how she would describe the room. And if she were a visitor at the B and B, this room was where she would request to stay. She'd select a book from inside the bench, curl up underneath the window and read the day away. And if Pamela had made any of her mouthwatering apple crisps, she'd beg the family for a few of those to enjoy while she allowed her mind to drift to another world.

No worries about money. No worries about sick children. No worries about gambling men.

She rubbed her eyes. The cleaning was taking longer than usual. She needed to put in her time, but she didn't want to hang around longer than necessary, either. So far, she hadn't run into Ben, and she didn't want to.

Deciding she'd have to take a quick break to have enough energy to finish, she sat in the wooden rocking chair and pulled a package of peanut butter crackers from her pocket. After eating a couple, she called Aunt Jane on the cell phone. "How's Pete?"

"He's doing fine. Have you talked to Ben?"

"No."

"Have you seen him?"

"No.

"Are you going to try to see him?

"No."

Aunt Jane sighed into the phone. "I didn't have a moment's peace last night, Maggie."

"That makes two of us."

"I just don't know that I should have told you. Maybe I misunderstood…"

"Aunt Jane, I know you don't like to say anything bad about anyone. But I needed to know that."

"It's just…"

"I've got to go. More work still to do. Give Pete a kiss for me. On the top of his head, anyway." She tried to laugh, but it sounded stilted in her own ears. "I'll see you in a bit."

Maggie threw the peanut butter wrapper in the trash in the yellow guest room bathroom then got to work cleaning it. Though she loved the yellow bedroom best of all, the connecting bathroom was by far her least favorite. White walls. White mats. White towels. And white wasn't always the easiest to clean. Even with bleach and elbow grease.

Just as she finished sweeping, her phone rang. She saw her mother's name on the screen and frowned. Mom never called during work hours. Hoping everything was all right with Mom and her sister, Maggie pushed the button. "Hello."

"Hi, Maggie. I just got off the phone with Aunt Jane."

Maggie rolled her eyes. Great. She had no doubt Aunt Jane had spilled about Ben and his less-than-becoming hobby. Now her mom knew what a foolish judge of character she was. Then again, maybe Aunt Jane hadn't said anything. Just in case, Maggie pretended ignorance. "Were you just checking on her? She seems to be doing great."

Maggie knew her voice sounded a pitch higher than usual, and her sentences shot out too fast.

"She called me."

Maggie cringed. So much for hoping Aunt Jane hadn't blabbed. "It's not a biggie, Mom."

"Yes, it is. You seemed to really like the guy, and Aunt Jane is feeling guilty for saying anything."

Maggie scratched her forehead then traced her fingers through her hair. "Mom, I really can't talk about this right now. I'm working."

"Okay, honey. But I want you to call me tonight."

"I'll try."

"I mean it. I better get a phone call."

Maggie blew her bangs away from her eyes. "Fine. I'll call you later."

"I love you."

"Love you, too." She clicked off the phone and shoved it in her front pocket. When she turned, she jumped to see Tammie standing behind her. She placed her hand against her chest. "Sorry. You scared me."

Tammie lifted her hands. "Didn't mean to. I just came to check and make sure everything was all right. You seemed really tired when you got here this morning."

"Pete was sick last night."

"Ben mentioned that. I hope he's all right."

Maggie gritted her teeth and nodded, hoping her expression didn't betray the fury she felt toward Tammie's youngest child. She hadn't told Ben about her dad's gambling addiction. The subject simply hadn't come up. Now she wondered if she'd mentioned it if she would have been able to see him for what he really was by his response.

"I'm assuming Jane has him."

Maggie nodded again.

"Well, the reason I came up here is I wanted to invite you to lunch with me, Callie and Pamela."

"I don't know if—"

"We'd love for you to go."

"It's just I wouldn't feel right—"

Tammie placed her hand on Maggie's arm. "You work so hard, Maggie. You need a break. Call Jane and see how Pete is doing."

Maggie shifted her weight from one foot to the other, trying to think of a way to get out of going with them. "I called Aunt Jane, and he's fine, but I'm pretty tired, and…"

"Then it's settled." She clasped her hands. "We'll be able to treat you to lunch then you can head home and take a nap."

"Well…"

"Come on," Tammie prodded. "It will be nice to go to lunch with all you girls."

All you girls. The words rolled around Maggie's mind. Tammie probably thought she and Ben had a thing going. Well, Maggie had thought so, too, until she learned the truth. Still, his family had been good to her. She wouldn't have been able to pay the bills as long as they had if not for this part-time job. "Okay. I'll go."

"Terrific. How much longer until you're done?"

"About fifteen minutes."

Tammie clapped her hands together as she looked around the room. "By the way, everything looks great."

Ben wiped sweaty hands against blue dress pants. The nasally secretary who'd called him for the interview looked exactly as he'd pictured her on the phone. Brown hair with gray streaks pulled back tight in some sort of bun. So tight that her eyes slanted beneath thick, brown-framed glasses. She wore a navy blue dress suit with a white ruffled shirt beneath the jacket. Though he hadn't seen her shoes yet, he would bet they were flat, brown loafers.

A buzzer sounded at her desk. She picked up the phone, then set it down. She looked at him. "Mr. Brown will see you now."

He stood, gripping his briefcase, which contained little more than a couple of extra copies of his résumé. "Thank you."

He walked into the oversize office, admiring the wall of windows behind the enormous oak desk. Built-in bookshelves lined the walls on both sides. Mr. Brown, who looked like the picture on the website, plus a few pounds, stood and extended his hand. "It's a pleasure to meet you, Ben Jacobs."

Ben shook his hand then took a seat when Mr. Brown motioned to it. The older gentleman placed his elbows on the table and clasped his hands. "So, Mr. Jacobs, tell me about yourself."

Ben shared about his family and living and going to church in Bloom Hollow.

"No wife?"

"Not yet, sir."

"Planning to stay in Bloom Hollow, are you?"

Ben shook his head. "Not if I get the job. I enjoyed living in Knoxville when I was at the University of Tennessee and I look forward to coming back."

The older man nodded then shared the expectations of the position. He talked about the other engineers in the company the new hire would work with. "So, tell me what type of designing you've done since leaving the university."

Trepidation washed over him, and Ben's hands clammed up. He tried not to wipe them on his pants. Heat rose under his collar, and he focused on not stretching his neck. "Well, since graduating I've been working on my family's farm. Operating machinery, yes. But I haven't made any designs."

Mr. Brown's eyebrows met in a line. "Not even just for your own pleasure?" He waved his hand. "An attempt to make something more efficient. In the home or on the farm."

Ben wanted to think of something. Come up with some machine he could at least say he'd worked on. But that would be a lie. He shook his head. "No, sir."

"Hmm." Mr. Brown lowered his gaze and wrote something on the paper in front of him.

Ben discreetly wiped his hands against his pants. If the man shook his hand now, he'd be completely disgusted.

"I called your references. They all gave glowing recommendations."

Ben smiled. "I'm glad, sir."

"I happen to be golf partners with one of the instructors at UT. I'm sure you remember Dr. Knoll."

Ben swallowed. Of all the professors in that huge school, Mr. Brown would be friends with the one who'd called Ben into his office and told him to get his act together or he wouldn't pass the class. He'd passed. Barely. "Yes, I do."

"I spoke with him, as well."

Ben waited for a response. Had Dr. Knoll slammed his character, or by some chance of mercy, said something positive about Ben? Mr. Brown didn't offer any clues, and Ben couldn't read his expression.

"Well, I believe that's all I need." He shuffled the papers on his desk then stuck them all in a manila folder. Ben noticed he had several other manila folders on his desk and wondered how many people were interviewing for the position. "Do you have any additional questions or comments for me?"

Please hire me. I need this job. I want to keep Maggie and Pete close. Don't want them to move to the other side of the state. "No." Ben stood, wiping his hands in one swift motion one last time on his pants. He extended his hand. "Thank you for meeting with me."

"We'll be in touch."

Ben walked out of the office. Amy Rogers sat in the seat he'd been in half an hour before. She was one of the top students in his class. She smiled and nodded, and Ben's heart sank. He didn't have a chance of getting the job if she was interviewing.

He barely made it out of the building when he had to take off the jacket and tie. No matter that the air was thick with cold January air. Ben was on fire.

He saw a deli across the street. Once inside, he ordered a toasted ham and cheese with potato chips and a pickle. He dropped into a chair, the weight of the lousy interview falling heavy upon him. *God, I was so sure last night. When I got the call, I just felt like this was going to be it. My big break.*

Now he felt as if he'd wasted a day driving to the city. Of course, the farm wasn't exactly hopping during the month of January. Aside from taking care of the animals and keeping the equipment and houses in good order, it wasn't as if the family dealt with a bunch of customers.

"Ben, I can't believe it's you."

Ben looked up and saw his college friend Taylor with a tray in his hand. He stood. "Sit across from me." When Taylor put down his tray, Ben gave him a quick, brotherly hug. "It's great to see you."

"Don't know if I believe that. You don't answer half my calls or texts."

They sat down and Ben said, "That's because I don't play poker anymore."

"I know." Taylor took a bite of his sandwich. "So, what you been up to? Interviewing, it looks like."

Ben flicked the collar of his shirt. "Yep. Had an interview today."

"How'd it go?"

"Not so great."

Taylor studied him for several seconds, and Ben took a bite of his sandwich then a drink of his Coke. "Why don't you come back to my place and see Jim?"

"You two share an apartment now?"

"Yeah. Just for now."

Ben didn't mention his surprise. Before they graduated, Jim had a steady girlfriend itching for an engagement ring. When Ben was a betting man, he would have put down good money that the two of them would be hitched within a month of graduation. But then he also remembered that Jim's attraction to the poker table mirrored Ben's a lot of the time.

Taylor interrupted his thoughts. "I know he'd love to see you."

Ben shook his head. "I'd better get back to the farm."

"It'll just be for a minute."

Ben chewed his bottom lip. He didn't need to go to Taylor's. Every time he'd gone over there he ended up in a game or a situation he couldn't get out of. He thought of Pastor Kent's advice to flee temptation.

But Taylor and Jim were his friends, and he hadn't seen them in a while. Besides, it wasn't even noon. What was the likelihood anything bad would happen? "Okay. But just for a minute."

Chapter 15

Maggie felt out of place sitting at the table with Tammie, Callie and Pamela. Not only were they Ben's family, but they were dressed in jeans and nice sweaters, while Maggie wore stretch pants and a sweatshirt. After cleaning the B and B, they'd given her time to run a brush through her hair, wash her face, even add a bit of mascara and light lipstick, but she still felt like she hadn't slept all night and had been cleaning all morning. Which she had.

Stifling a yawn, she picked through her salad with her fork. She ached over Ben. If he walked into the restaurant at this moment, her heart would drum and her stomach would churn with excitement. And she hated that. Hated that she still felt so strongly for a man who was like her father.

Callie brushed a stray lock of blond hair behind her ear. Long, brown, beaded earrings hung from her lobes. Normally, Maggie would think the accessory way too big, especially on a woman as petite as Callie, but these complemented her light, creamy complexion and enhanced the bright color of her eyes. With apparent ease, Callie folded one leg under her, still not making her quite as tall as Pamela, who sat in the seat beside her. It amazed Maggie to think the woman had been able to carry two babies in such a small frame. Callie looked at Pamela. "So, how's the job search going?"

Pamela swallowed a spoonful of soup then dabbed her mouth with her napkin. Maggie hadn't realized it before, but Pamela must have just gotten her hair cut. Chestnut highlights streaked through choppy red locks that barely touched her shoulders. "Actually, I haven't applied yet."

Tammie put down her fork. "What? But I thought you had several places you were looking into."

"I did." Pamela wrapped her fingers around the charm on her necklace. "But the jobs were all in Knoxville, and Jack and I talked about it, and I'm not sure I'd want to commute."

"It's not that far. Only forty-five minutes," said Tammie.

"I know, but that's ninety minutes on the road each day." She shrugged. "The girls love their schools, and we love our new house." A slow grin lifted her lips. "I might just have to stay on as the Jacobs's family accountant and live in Bloom Hollow."

Callie wrapped her arm around Pamela's shoulder. "You'll hear no complaints from me about that."

"Me, either," agreed Tammie.

Callie looked at Maggie. "So, how's your aunt Jane doing? I don't get to see her as much now that she has you to help her."

"She's doing well. High blood pressure is under control, and believe it or not, it seems having a four-year-old in the house helps her."

Tammie nodded. "I'm sure she loves having Pete around. Jane has always been so good with the children."

"I miss her," Callie added.

"Come over anytime. I know she'd love to see you," said Maggie.

Callie nodded. "Every time I went to her house, she'd have me rolling about something someone said or did at the beauty parlor. And that hat. How many ribbons does she have for that straw hat?"

"More than my sister and I had combined as little girls," laughed Maggie.

"She's quite a character," said Pamela.

"Definitely a lot of fun," Tammie added.

Their conversation last night sure hadn't been a lot of fun. It wasn't Aunt Jane's fault, and she knew the woman stewed over whether she should have told Maggie. But even though the truth hurts sometimes doesn't mean the words shouldn't be said. And Maggie had to know.

"Speaking of fun, I enjoy having Pete in children's church," said Pamela.

Maggie chuckled as she swallowed a bite of salad. "He loves his Sunday church as he calls it. It's good for him to have that time with kids, since he's always stuck with grown-ups."

Pamela leaned forward. "Last Sunday we were talking about when Jesus walked on water. One of the little girls asked how Jesus could do that, and Pete popped up out of his chair and exclaimed, 'Like this,' then he held out his arms and tiptoed around the room." Pamela cupped her hand over her mouth when she started to laugh. "But the funniest part was he sucked in a deep breath, puffed out his cheeks and held his breath as he walked around."

Callie giggled. "I guess Jesus had to hold his breath when walking on water."

Pamela dabbed her eyes. "That's what was so funny."

Maggie's heart warmed as she pictured her sweet boy learning about Jesus and trying to picture Him in his young mind. "That sounds like Pete."

"He's such a good boy," added Pamela. "Full of energy."

Maggie chortled. "You're not kidding. I'm not sure that boy knows how to walk."

"I believe I heard Ben say the same thing," said Tammie.

Maggie stiffened at the mention of his name. She crossed her legs and shifted in her seat.

"Ben sure is crazy about that boy," she added.

Maggie nodded and took a bite of her salad so she wouldn't have to respond.

"It's true," said Callie. "He talks about Pete all the time. What he did or what he said." She twirled her fork in the air. "'Course that shouldn't be a surprise. He's always been crazy about his nieces and nephews."

"True," said Tammie, "I'd always thought Ben wasn't ready to be around children all the time, but…"

Maggie sucked in her breath as a wave of nausea washed over her. Callie must have noticed Maggie's panic because she interrupted Tammie. "Where is Ben? I haven't seen him today."

"Had to go to Knoxville."

Maggie jumped out of her chair. "Excuse me." She pressed her fingers against her mouth. "I hope I haven't caught Pete's bug."

She raced toward the bathroom as Aunt Jane's words about Ben's plan to join a game filtered through her mind. He must be going today. How could she have been so foolish? She splashed water on her face then stared at her reflection. Well, she wasn't now. And she wouldn't be ever again.

Ben's heart pounded against his chest as he followed Taylor up the stairs to his apartment. His mind whirred and his hands grew clammy when he thought of the last time he'd been there. And lost money. A lot of money.

Taylor pulled keys out of his pocket and unlocked the door. "Jimmy, look who I brought home with me?"

Ben walked inside, and his college buddy jumped off the couch then smacked his hand against his thigh and howled. Jimmy looked the same. Reddish hair, a bit too long, old wrinkled T-shirt, baggy jeans. He grabbed his friend's hand then wrapped his other arm around his shoulder. "How ya been, Jimmy?"

Jimmy raked his fingers through his hair. "I'm doing all right."

"How's Tanya?" asked Ben.

Jimmy's face paled, and he glanced at the door behind Ben. "Got a job in Indiana. Haven't talked to her in months."

"And he don't need her." Taylor patted Jimmy's shoulder. "Right, man?"

Jimmy laughed, a forced sound, and Ben noted the sadness in his college friend's eyes. Jimmy pointed to the table. "You're just in time, man."

Ben froze when he saw the cards and poker chips. His stomach clenched. "I just came by to say hello."

"You gotta stay, man," said Jimmy. "We need a fourth player."

Ben tried to laugh, but his mouth suddenly felt thick. Parched. "I only see three of us."

"Ben," a voice called down the hall. "It's great to see you."

Rick Mason. Wow, he looked different. Rick had been clean-cut. Smart. A go-getter. Now he wore a dirty button-down work shirt and old jeans. His hair was longer than Ben had ever seen, and it had been a while since the guy had shaved.

"Rick?" Ben shook his hand. "It's great to see you. What have you been up to?"

He wrinkled his nose. "Work mostly."

"Still dating Sabrina?"

Pain flashed across Rick's features, and he shook his head. "Nah."

Ben swallowed the knot in his throat, remembering how Taylor told him Rick had to drop out of school. So, Rick and Jimmy had both lost their girlfriends. In Ben's estimation they'd been crazy about those women. He'd always figured they'd end up married. Ben pointed to the company name on Rick's shirt. "Just get off work?"

"Nah. Just my lunch hour." He rubbed his hands together and looked at Taylor and Jimmy. "We gonna get this game going or not? Some of us have to be back at work soon."

Ben's jaw slacked. "You took your lunch hour to play poker?"

"Just a quick game."

Taylor sat at the table shuffling cards. "Come on, boys. Have a seat. Let's get started."

Ben sat across from Taylor. His hands started to sweat, and his head swam as Taylor dealt the cards. Jimmy and Rick picked up their cards. Ben stared at his lying face-down in front of him. His brain, his spirit, seemed to scream for him to get up and run, not walk, but run out of the apartment. He licked his lips and rubbed his thumbs against his fingertips, but oh, how he wanted to pick up those cards. Just for a second. Just to see what he'd been dealt.

Maggie's face filled his mind. Then Pete's. They meant so much to him. More than the momentary satisfaction of a poker game. Even a poker win. He stood and took his keys out of his pocket. "Sorry, guys. I've got to go."

They groaned and mumbled, but Ben waved and walked out of the apartment.

Relief swept over him like a soothing balm as he made his way to the car. He drove straight to the homeless shelter where his brother-in-law worked. Jack greeted him at the door, and they walked back to his office. "So, how'd the interview go?"

"Awful. I'm sure I didn't get the job."

Jack frowned. "I'm sorry, man."

Ben shook his head then gripped his hair with both hands. "I don't even care." He brought his hands down, rubbing his cheeks and jaw. "I just said no to a poker game."

"Wait." Jack lifted his hand and motioned for Ben to have a seat. "A poker game? Why would you be anywhere near a poker game?"

Ben flopped onto the couch while Jack settled into the chair behind his desk. He understood the concern wrapping his brother-in-law's expression. Ben hadn't realized the draw to gamble had been so tight, so desperate. He hadn't had as much trouble saying no to the game in Bloom Hollow, because he wasn't near anyone who gambled. But being in the same room with cards and chips... A tremble shot through his body. The urge had been so strong.

He told Jack about seeing Taylor at the deli and agreeing to go to the apartment to say hello to Jim. He pointed to his chest. "I knew I wasn't supposed to go. I could feel it."

Jack didn't say anything, but listened as Ben continued about seeing Rick and the cards and sitting at the table and how desperately he wanted to play. So much so he could taste it.

"Which is why we flee temptation. I can't go anywhere near a liquor store. And you shouldn't go anywhere near a poker game."

"You're right." Ben leaned back on the couch and stared up at the ceiling. "I wish I hadn't gone to that apartment. I knew I should have turned him down back at the deli."

Jack stood and moved around the desk and sat on the edge of it. "Ben, did you play?"

"No."

"All right, then. Quit beating yourself up. The temptation was great. God was there with you, and you said no."

Ben sat up again. "Yeah, but I wanted to play. Bad."

Jack leaned forward. "But you didn't. And now you know why it's so important to stay completely away from the game."

Ben looked at his brother-in-law. "It took me a long time to forgive you."

"I know." Sorrow flashed through Jack's eyes. "I lost eight years with my wife and daughters because of the bottle."

Ben remembered. Pamela had been a good mom, but she'd grown cold and bitter. The girls were well taken care of with his parents, him and Kirk to be additional support for his sister. But no one really replaces a dad.

Jack actually ended up on the streets, homeless, before he accepted Christ, cleaned up his act, finished school then came back to Tennessee to reunite with his family. Pamela hadn't been easy to convince that he'd changed. Ben hadn't been easy, either.

"All those times I was angry with you," said Ben. "I didn't realize I was becoming like you, just with a different vice."

Jack placed his hand on Ben's shoulder. "But you've given yours over to God early on. You're not going to lose eight years."

He thought of Maggie and Pete. He cared for them. Wanted to protect them. Help them. Love them. "No, I'm not."

Ben stood and shook Jack's hand. "Thanks for listening, man."

"Anytime. And if you don't get that job, God will provide another."

"I know." Ben cringed as he walked out of the room. He didn't think there was any *if* about it. There was no way he'd be offered the job.

Chapter 16

Maggie groaned despite Pete's cheers from the back-seat as she pulled into the Jacobs's driveway. She should have just said no when Tammie invited her, Aunt Jane and Pete to dinner. But Tammie had been so good to them, and she just hadn't had the heart to decline.

She knew the whole family would be there. Callie had been excited about the boys and Pete getting to play to-gether. And Pamela assured her the girls would keep the three of them out of trouble. Ben would act as if nothing happened. In his mind, nothing had happened. He didn't know she'd found out about his gambling.

"I'll take Pete inside if you'll carry the baked beans. My hands are a bit sore today," said Aunt Jane.

"No problem." Maggie glanced at her aunt's hands. Her knuckles were swollen more than usual, and it pained Maggie to think how much discomfort they must cause her aunt. She grabbed the dish and made her way to the house.

"You're here." Tammie welcomed each of them with a smile and a hug.

Maggie placed the beans on the counter then had to practically hold Pete down to pull off his coat. "Hang on, son."

Pete twisted. "I'm gonna play wit Ronald and Teddy."

"Not if I can't get you out of this coat," she said.

Her son broke free of the outerwear, and Maggie placed the coat on the back of a chair. She smiled at Mike and Tammie. "Thanks for inviting us."

"No problem at all." Tammie swatted the air. "You and Pete and Jane are practically family."

Maggie's stomach twisted, and she exhaled a long breath to slow her racing heart. She'd have been ready to jump on the chance to be part of this family. How she loved them. Hearing Pete's cackles from a few rooms away, her son was smitten with them, as well.

"Smells good." Mike sniffed the beans then rubbed his stomach.

Tammie patted his arm. "Give us five minutes then we'll have everything ready."

Callie and Pamela took dishes from the stove and placed them on the dining room table. Kirk hefted plates out of the cabinet, while Jack pulled out the silverware.

"How can I help?" asked Maggie.

"There's not a thing you can do." Tammie snapped her fingers. "Actually, you can go get Ben from the cabin. Tell him we're ready."

Maggie's heart sank. "Why don't I get the dishes, and Kirk can run over there?"

Kirk winked. "'Cause he'd rather see you."

Unable to come up with a response, Maggie nodded.

She slipped back into her coat and silently prayed as she buttoned it. Talking to Ben didn't have to be a big deal. Maybe she wouldn't have to see him at all. She could knock on the door, holler that the food was ready, then head back to the house. An idea came to her and she turned to Tammie as she pulled out her cell phone. "I'll just call him."

Tammie shook her head. "We've tried for half an hour. He's there. The car and the truck are here. He just won't pick up."

Maggie headed to his cabin. *Please, God, I don't want to yell at him, or cry, or fall more in love with him.* She squeezed her eyes shut at the last thought. Last night she'd felt convinced that her mom and aunt were right, that they'd have to move. She knew Aunt Jane didn't really want to leave, but the bills continued to pile up and Maggie couldn't stay around Ben, either. She'd almost given in to the idea that she'd been wrong to try to save the house and shop all along. *Then why did Aunt Jane ask me to come and help her?*

She knocked on the door and Ben yelled, "Come on in. I'm almost ready."

Maggie warred within herself. Should she just holler "food's ready" and head back to the house? Inhaling a deep breath to steady her thoughts, she stepped inside and said, "Ben."

She heard a hair dryer blowing from down the hall and stifled a grin as she wondered how many men used a hair dryer. Not Paul. But then he'd had a military buzz cut the entire time they'd been married.

His phone beeped from the coffee table. She glanced toward it and the screen lit up with Poker Bud at the top. The message read Why'd you leave so soon?

Fury swept through Maggie. He was a fool. Gambling

took away everything. Money. Security. Family. And she was a fool for not having seen who he was. Suddenly, she didn't mind running into Ben. In fact, she demanded the confrontation.

She stomped down the hall and banged on the door. "Ben, I need to talk to you."

He opened the door, his eyes twinkling with delight, and for the briefest moment, Maggie wanted to wrap her arms around him. Common sense took over, and she pursed her lips. "I want you to know that I do not want anything to do with you. Do not come to the house to see me. Do not seek me out while I'm working at the B and B. And do not ask to take my son anywhere ever again."

He furrowed his brows. "Maggie? What happened?"

"I'll tell you what happened. I was an idiot. I should have seen the signs." She smacked her hand against her forehead. "I still can't remember any signs. That's how foolish I am."

"What are you talking about?"

"It doesn't matter. Just leave Pete and me alone." She turned to leave. "Oh, and dinner is ready."

Maggie stormed out of the cabin. She wasn't ready to be with Ben's family yet. She never should have said they'd come. Stomping to the activity center, she pressed her hands against the fence. Remembering the fun she and Ben had playing that day weighed on her heart heavier than the mounting bills with no income in sight.

She threw back her head and looked up at the clear blue sky. The air was cold, crisp. They hadn't had a good snow yet, just a few days of sprinklings. But the time was coming. Soon. She could feel it. As hot and angry as she felt right now, she needed the cool temperature to settle the pounding in her heart and head.

Why did she still find him so attractive? The look of

A Love Discovered

confusion and hurt in his eyes had tugged at her, making her want to touch his cheek and tell him everything would be okay. Well, everything was not okay.

The cold air finally seeped through, and she grabbed the collar of her coat and dipped her chin inside. Sadness already warred to take over her anger, and hot tears brimmed her eyelids. She didn't want to cry. Couldn't. How would she explain it to Ben's family? *I just have to get through the dinner. I can do this.*

Ben slipped on his loafers and grabbed his coat out of the closet. He had no idea what Maggie was upset about. His mind replayed the last time he'd seen her. He'd invited her and Pete to dinner, then Pete got sick. Nothing. He couldn't think of a single thing he'd done or said that would upset her so much.

He flew out of the cabin. He didn't want to talk to her in front of the family, but what choice did he have? Out of the corner of his eye, he spied someone standing beside the activity center. Maggie.

Bounding toward her, he slowed when he saw her wipe her eyes with the back of her hand. His heart ached. "Maggie? What is it?"

"I saw the message on your phone."

He reached into his empty pocket, wishing he'd thought to pick up his phone off the table. "What message?"

She flipped around to face him, lifted both hands and made quotation gestures. "From 'Poker Bud.' He wanted to know why you left early." She smacked her hand against the fence. "You're a gambler?"

He blew out a breath, knowing he should have talked to her sooner. "I have had a gambling problem."

Her eyes lit with fire and pain. "Do you know what

gambling has done in my life? My dad gambled. He lost money, at times to the point we weren't sure where we'd get money for groceries or clothes for school. Ultimately, he lost his family." She lifted both palms in the air. "I haven't seen or spoken with my dad since I was fifteen. I don't even know if he's still alive."

Ben felt each word like a blow to the stomach. He ached for the pain he saw in her face. Hurt for the man he could have become. And the reality of what could happen if he didn't stay away from the game. He reached for her hands, but she pulled away. "Maggie, listen, I haven't played in eight months. Not since May. I have a problem. I know that, but…"

She shook her head. "Aunt Jane heard you making plans. The day Pete got sick."

He furrowed his brows, trying to think why Jane would have thought that.

"You were in the hall, and you said 'game on.'"

Realization dawned, and he opened his mouth to respond, but Maggie pointed to the cabin and continued, "And I saw the message from your friend. How can you deny—"

"Maggie." He reached for her hands again and caught the right one. She yanked back, but he held tight. "Listen, what your aunt heard was me being excited because I'd gotten a job interview. I went to Knoxville yesterday because of that. Not for a poker game."

Maggie snapped her lips shut and frowned. He knew she was trying to decide whether she could believe him. She shook her head. "But your phone?"

"It was a horrible interview. I went to a deli across the street for lunch, and I ran into a college friend. His name is 'Poker Bud' in my phone." With his free hand, he scratched his jaw. "I should block his calls altogether.

I've wanted to keep contact. Thought maybe I could be a witness to him."

She cocked her head, crossed her arms in front of her chest and pushed out her hip. With an incredulous tone, she retorted, "So you didn't play cards?"

"No."

He stared into her eyes, waiting for the word to sink in, praying his gaze shone with complete sincerity. She averted her gaze, and her stonelike stance softened. He reached for her other hand, and she didn't pull back. His heart raced with what he knew had to be said. "But I want to be honest with you. He asked me to his apartment to see another friend. When I got there, they were starting a game. I can't deny I wanted to play, but I didn't. With God's help, I walked out of there."

Maggie stared at him. Her gaze seemed to beg to know if he was telling the truth and yet she hesitated to believe him. He wanted to assure her he'd been honest, held nothing back, but she'd have to believe him herself. He couldn't decide for her. She looked down at the ground. "You have no idea how hard things were when Dad started gambling."

He took a step toward her, wanting to wrap her in his arms and promise he would never hurt her or Pete. "I'm sorry, Maggie. I didn't know about your dad. I should have told you about my past, about—"

She pulled her hands away and glared up at him. "Yes, you should have."

"Maggie, I'm sorry."

She lifted her hand. "I don't want to talk anymore. I need time to think."

She stomped away from him. He considered going after her then decided he'd give her time. All those times he'd thought he should tell her about his battle, and he never did. *Well, God, it appears I've flubbed up a job prospect and my relationship with Maggie.*

His heart ached, but he couldn't despair. She'd gone into the house and hadn't come out to leave with Pete and her aunt. They'd get through dinner. He would give her time to think, and he would pray. He might even get the family to pray with him.

He made his way to the house. When he saw Pete, the four-year-old squealed and raced to him. Ben tousled his hair and glanced at Maggie to see how she would respond. She sat still, pretending not to notice her son's exuberance at seeing him.

She wasn't going to make a scene. Good. He lifted Pete underneath his arms and spun him around. "It's good to see you, little buddy."

"We came to eat dinner."

"I know."

"Can I sit wif you?"

"Of course."

Pete wrapped his arms around Ben's neck. "I love you, Mr. Ben."

Ben looked at Maggie. She stared at him and Pete with a look of sadness that almost knocked him off his feet. He kissed the boy's forehead. "I love you, too, Pete. So very much."

He placed Pete on the floor and gazed again at Maggie. The look in her eyes ripped his heart to shreds. Sometimes love wasn't enough.

Chapter 17

"He admitted he has a problem."

Maggie poured her aunt a cup of coffee. She'd had another long, sleepless night. She couldn't remember when she'd felt so weary, not even when Pete was a baby and she was dealing with Paul's death. She'd had no control over those circumstances, but with Ben...she could choose to love him or not. Well, maybe she couldn't change her feelings, but she could control her actions.

Aunt Jane poured creamer into her cup. "I'm sorry, honey. What did he say?"

"That he hasn't played a game in eight months. That he's quit."

"But?"

"He said that what you heard was his excitement at getting a job interview."

Aunt Jane shook her head. "I should have just asked him right then and there." She blew on the coffee then took a sip. "Could that be true? Do young people say 'game on' when they get job interviews?"

Maggie grinned at her aunt's innocent tone. The woman didn't want to think poorly of Ben, but she didn't want Maggie and Pete hurt, either. "It's possible."

"Oh, dear." Her aunt rubbed her swollen knuckles.

"Do you need some painkiller?"

"Already took some." She lifted both fists and winked. "That boy better not be lying, or me and my Muhammad Ali fists will take him down the next time I see him."

Maggie chuckled at her aunt's attempt to lighten the conversation. She buttered her toast then added some grape jelly. She was thankful she wouldn't be working at the Jacobs's farm today, just the consignment shop. She needed some time to digest all Ben had said. Her heart wanted to believe him. Every word. But how would she know he was being honest? And even if he was, he admitted to having a problem, and she wasn't sure she wanted to take a chance he'd start up again.

"Mom!" Pete yelled from the bathroom.

"Oh, boy," Maggie muttered.

"Hope you don't have to *hurl* yourself back there." Aunt Jane nudged Maggie's elbow. "Get it?"

Maggie shook her head. "Yes. I get it."

"Mom!" Pete hollered again.

She walked into the bathroom and released a sigh when he only needed help with the string around his pajama pants. She tousled his hair. "Morning, big guy." She helped him finish up and wash his hands. "You ready for breakfast?"

He gave an exaggerated nod then raced to the kitchen. "Hi, Aunt Jane." His voice boomed.

As she washed her own hands, she grinned at her aunt's soft reminder that Pete use his inside voice. She fixed him a bowl of cereal and poured a small glass of juice then set them on the table.

Pete took a bite of his food, his little legs swinging back and forth at the edge of the chair. Milk dripped down his chin and he licked it off. "Is Mr. Ben coming over today?"

Maggie looked at Aunt Jane, who continued to rub her knuckles though Maggie wondered if the gesture was as much from anxiety as pain. She shook her head at the child. "No, Pete. Not today."

"Are we going to eat at his house again today?"

"No." She patted his hand. "Eat your breakfast."

Pete pounded his elbows against the table then dropped his chin onto his fists. "I want to see Mr. Ben."

Of all days for him to behave this way. She had no desire to deal with her own warring feelings as well as her son's temper tantrum. "Well, I'm sorry, Pete, but you're not going to see him today."

His bottom lip quivered, and his eyes brimmed with tears. Frustration gurgled up inside of Maggie.

Aunt Jane pointed to one of the marshmallow pieces in Pete's cereal. "Well, lookie there, Pete. It's green. Isn't that your favorite color?"

Distracted, Pete leaned forward, picked up the marshmallow and popped it into his mouth. He giggled when Aunt Jane gasped and pressed her hand against her chest. "You've done it now."

"Done what?" asked Pete.

Aunt Jane pointed a curled finger toward his face. "The green is already spreading on your cheeks. I've told you before that color is catching."

Pete snorted as he raced toward the bathroom to check his face. "I'm not green. You're silly."

The phone rang, and Maggie answered it while her aunt made her way out of the kitchen. "Hello."

"Hi, Maggie. This is Carl Pearson."

Maggie gripped the back of the chair. This might be the answer to her prayer. If he'd decided to buy the house and shop, then they'd move. She and Pete wouldn't stay in Bloom Hollow. God was taking the decision out of her hands. She glanced toward the hall and saw her aunt leaning against the jamb between the kitchen and hall. Her chest tightened. She didn't want her aunt to lose her home, either.

"Hello?"

His voice sounded over the line, and Maggie gasped. "I'm so sorry. Hello, Carl. How were your holidays?"

"Very nice. Thank you for asking, but I wanted to call about the property."

"Yes?"

Maggie thought about all the work that would go into packing up the house and the consignment store. She wondered what would be the best way to sell the items in the shop. If she could find all of her aunt's records, she could return the shop items back to their original owners. If they'd take them back.

"I've decided not to buy the property."

"What?"

Maggie had been so sure he'd make an offer. Originally, she'd planned to refuse him, or at least try to talk him out of it. But after the past few days, she'd just been sure God wanted to get her and Pete away from Ben.

"I've decided on some other property, but thank you for letting me view your place. It's very nice."

"Are you…are you sure?"

"Yes. I don't suppose I would joke about something like this."

Maggie's cheeks warmed. "Of course not. I just thought… I mean, I was sure you liked our place."

"I did, but I decided on something else."

"Well, thank you for calling."

Maggie hung up and sat back in the chair. Pete had already climbed back in his seat and started eating his cereal again. She looked at Aunt Jane. "That was Carl Pearson."

"Not interested, I take it."

Maggie shook her head. Her emotions were nothing short of complete confusion. She wanted to get away from Ben. She didn't want to get away from Ben. She wanted to keep the house and shop for Aunt Jane. She didn't know how to keep the house and shop for Aunt Jane. Chewing the inside of her mouth, she wondered if she could take a vacation from her mind.

"We'll find someone," said Aunt Jane.

Noting the disappointment in her aunt's expression, Maggie gripped the edge of the table with both hands. "I'll find a way for you to keep your house, Aunt Jane."

"Maggie," she said, "I do not mind moving."

She said the words, but Maggie saw sadness in her eyes. Never in a million years would her aunt admit her true feelings, and Maggie wasn't a quitter. She would find a way to keep the property. And stay away from Ben Jacobs.

Ben brought the ax down, connecting blade to wood. The log split apart. He picked up the two pieces and tossed them in the wheelbarrow. Picking up another piece, he repeated the process. His chest and arms burned from the exertion, and sweat dotted his forehead despite the freezing temperature. But he didn't care. The pain and cold reminded him he was still alive.

He hadn't gotten the job, and Maggie hadn't talked to him in weeks. He tried to focus on the farm. Jack stopped by the cabin most evenings to encourage him and share Scriptures. Ben strived to trust God, and he'd never felt so close to his heavenly Father. And yet, he ached for Maggie and Pete. And he longed for an engineering job, for the chance to make his own way, stand on his own two feet.

"Working hard?" Ben turned and saw his dad walking toward him. He handed Ben a thermos then buttoned the top of his coat. "Son, it's freezing out here."

Ben swiped his forehead with the back of his hand then took the drink. "Not if you're working hard." He lifted the thermos. "Coffee?"

"Hot chocolate. Mom thought you'd like it."

Ben chuckled and took a slow sip, the drink warming him all the way to his toes. He nodded to the filled wheelbarrow. "Guess I've been working a little harder than I thought."

Dad pointed to the stacks of wood lined up against the back of the house. "Son, I think you've been working more than a little." He took the ax and planted the blade into the cutting log. "Let's take a little break. Head over to the cabin."

He'd been so wrapped up in his thoughts, he hadn't realized how much he'd chopped. Following his dad to the cabin, his mind whirred with possibilities of other things he could accomplish today. Maybe head over to the homeless shelter and help Jack for a while. Or check on the twins. Callie might need a break for an hour or two. Ben just had to stay busy.

They walked into the cabin and peeled off their coats. His dad settled onto the couch, and Ben sat across from him in the recliner.

"Office Incorporated's got a job opening," said Dad.

"I saw that," said Ben. Office Incorporated had been the last place Ben would have ever considered working. An engineer for the small Bloom Hollow company did little more than technician work on copiers, printers and other office equipment. He would have no opportunity for design or advancement. He'd simply go from one office to another and fix their equipment. Not what he hoped for in a position.

"Have you thought about applying?"

Ben shrugged. He liked the idea of staying closer to home, especially now that he had the cabin. And he wanted to be near Maggie. "I guess the experience would be helpful on my résumé."

"And it would keep you close to home."

Ben assumed his dad had a couple of motives for wanting him to stay home. First, Ben helped with the farm. Second, he wasn't as tempted to gamble in Bloom Hollow. Ben couldn't deny both were good reasons. "I'll probably apply."

"Great." His dad clasped his hands. "But that wasn't really why I wanted to talk with you. Do you remember your great-aunt Evelyn?"

Ben furrowed his brows. "No. I don't think so."

"She passed away when you were about six. Only came to visit a few times, but she always thought you were such a cute kid. Wild, but cute."

Ben grinned. "Smart woman."

Dad shoved his hand into his jacket pocket. "Well, Aunt Evelyn didn't have any kids. She and my uncle Alfred were married fifteen years when he passed away, and she never remarried."

"Okay." Ben scratched the stubble on his jaw. He had

no idea where his dad was going with the family history story.

Dad pulled a small black box out of his pocket and handed it to Ben. "She gave me this before she passed away."

Ben opened the box. Inside was a wedding ring set. The engagement ring had a round center diamond placed in a white gold square setting. On each side were two smaller diamonds then two even smaller diamonds beside each of those. The rest of the band was yellow gold, just like the plain wedding ring. He'd never seen a set like it, not that he'd ever done any wedding ring shopping, but the set was obviously unique. He handed it back to his dad. "It's really nice, Dad."

His dad pushed it back toward him. "I want you to have it."

Ben blinked. "What?"

"For Maggie."

Ben shook his head and tried to hand the box to his dad again. "No, Dad. Really. You can take it back. Maggie doesn't care about me. She won't even speak to me."

Dad grinned. "She loves you, Ben."

"You don't understand. Her dad was a gambler. He hurt their family."

Surprise then understanding wrapped his dad's features. "That's why…"

"That's why she doesn't want anything to do with me."

"So she knows…"

Ben leaned back his head then rubbed the back of his neck. "I was going to tell her, but she found out on her own. Which didn't go over so well."

His dad wrinkled his nose. "I bet it didn't." His dad grabbed the box out of Ben's hand. "Welp, there's no reason to give you this. You won't need it."

"Dad." Ben lifted his hands. "Aren't you supposed to tell me that I shouldn't give up? That God could change her heart? That if I love her..."

"Do you love her?"

"Yeah." Ben looked down at his hands then back at his dad. "I really do."

Dad smiled as he shoved the box back in Ben's hand. "Then don't give up. God *can* change her heart. And when He does, you can give this to her."

Ben looked at the rings again. They were perfect. If he'd gone to the jewelry store, he wouldn't have found a nicer set. He handed the box back to his dad. "I can't take this."

"Why not?"

"I didn't buy it. I don't even remember my great-aunt Evelyn."

"She would have been your great-great-aunt Evelyn," said Dad. He placed the box on the coffee table. "But you are going to take it."

"Dad."

He shook his head. "Aunt Evelyn wanted her rings to be passed down to her children, but God didn't allow her and Alfred to have any, so she gave them to me to pass on to one of my kids. You want to know why I want you to have them?"

"Why?"

"Great-Uncle Alfred had been a wild man, drinking, carousing, gambling, until he found the Lord and Evelyn. Then he changed." He patted the top of the box. "You, my son, have allowed God and a beautiful woman to change you."

Ben swallowed the knot in his throat. The ring was perfect, and he was going to win Maggie's heart.

Chapter 18

Maggie woke up and looked out the window. Just as the meteorologist predicted, it had snowed. A lot. The backyard looked like a winter wonderland with snow weighing the tree limbs and drifts pressed against the garage. Placing her feet against the hardwood floor, she shivered and pulled fluffy socks out of the drawer. After putting them on and then wrapping up in her shaggy pink robe, she padded to the kitchen and started the coffee.

She heard something scratching outside the house, and she frowned. She peeked through the window blinds and gasped. Ben scooped a large pile of snow into a shovel then dumped it into the yard. As if sensing her presence, he turned toward the window. Spying her, he smiled and waved.

Maggie shut the blinds and pressed her hand against her chest. She lifted her hand to the side of her head, knowing her hair stood at every imaginable angle. Why was he shoveling their snow? She hadn't spoken to him in weeks. Ignored him at every turn.

Of course, he still claimed her thoughts. Her aunt's house and consignment shop had to be cleaner than they'd ever been as she'd scoured every corner, crack and crevice. She'd cooked more casseroles and baked more desserts than she had in her life. Anything to try to keep her mind off Ben. And the piling debt.

"Who's outside?" asked Aunt Jane.

"Ben."

Her aunt frowned. "What's he doing?"

"Shoveling snow."

Aunt Jane clasped her hands and let out a little sigh. "What a sweet young man. Maggie, I'm afraid I might have spoken too soon. He…"

"Aunt Jane, we've talked about this. He has a problem."

"But…"

Maggie lifted her hand. "Aunt Jane, what can I get you for breakfast?"

Aunt Jane waved her toward the kitchen. "You go fix yourself what you want. I'm going to ask Ben to come inside so I can speak a word or two with him."

"Aunt Jane."

"You're not my boss, Maggie."

Maggie grinned at her aunt's words, and the way she stomped her foot and placed her hand on her hip.

Aunt Jane winked. "Now, you can stay here and talk to Ben with me, or you can go get your breakfast."

Maggie turned on her heels and sped to the kitchen. She tried to focus on pouring cereal into a bowl, but she could hear Aunt Jane thanking Ben for his help. She heard his deep voice from just outside the door, and butterflies flittered around her stomach.

"Mommy, who's here?" Pete walked into the kitchen, wiping his eyes with the back of his hands.

"No one…"

Ben's voice sounded again, and Pete's mouth dropped open and his eyes lit with excitement. "It's Mr. Ben."

Before Maggie could stop him, Pete raced out of the living room and toward the front door. She heard Aunt Jane invite Ben in for a cup of coffee, and Maggie started toward her bedroom. She'd hide as long as necessary.

"Hi, Maggie."

Maggie pulled the robe tighter around her waist and turned toward the man who refused to leave her thoughts. His eyes danced with amusement, and she reached a hand to her hair. How she wished she'd looked in a mirror before she'd stepped out of the bedroom. Brushed her teeth, even. "Hello, Ben." She bowed and said, "If you'll excuse me."

Running into the bathroom, she shut the door behind her. She'd bowed, actually bowed to him. What was she thinking?

Staring at her reflection, she released a groan. Her hair was worse than she'd thought. Flat on the left side. Completely flat. She even had creases on the left side of her forehead and cheek from the pillow. The right side of her hair stood up higher than Albert Einstein's frizzy mane.

She'd just stay in the bathroom until he left. She shook her head as she squeezed toothpaste onto the toothbrush. She scrubbed her teeth and then flossed, then washed her face and brushed her hair. Leaning her ear against the door, her heart skipped at Ben's deep laugh. How long was the guy planning to stay?

Maggie flopped onto the toilet seat cover and tightened the belt of the robe. Her stomach rumbled, and she wished he would hurry up and leave so she could start her day.

"I can't wait till I can ride Princess again," Pete practically yelled.

Ben responded, but she couldn't quite make out his words. She crossed her legs and twisted her foot left and right. The man needed to leave already.

"Aww, Mr. Ben, do you have to go?" Pete yelled several minutes later.

Maggie hopped up and pressed her ear against the door. She heard the front door open and shut then she walked out of the bathroom. Pete raced toward her and wrapped his arms around her waist. "Mommy, you missed Mr. Ben."

"I did," said Maggie. "That's too bad."

"No, it's all right," said Aunt Jane. "I invited him to dinner to thank him for shoveling the sidewalk."

Maggie's jaw dropped. "What?"

Aunt Jane pointed to the small parking area beside the consignment store. "He'd already cleared off the parking lot. I'd imagine dinner is the least we could do."

Maggie clamped her lips shut. She could think of plenty of other things they could do. Send him a card. Give him a gift certificate. Take him a pie. None of them included spending an evening with him. "I suppose I'll have to make myself scarce," said Maggie.

Aunt Jane shook her head. "Nope. I told him you'd make chicken and dumplings, since you've gotten the knack of it."

Great. Not only would she have to spend the evening with him, she'd have to spend the whole day cooking a meal she'd gotten right one time. No pressure at all.

Ben accepted the position with Office Incorporated, and he hated it. *Hate* might be too strong a word, but the duties included all that he'd expected. He spent each day fixing copiers, printers, projectors and even a few computers. Most of the time, the operator of the machine simply forgot to check all the cords or needed to change a light. Simple, boring stuff. No imagination necessary. But he was getting experience, and he still lived near Maggie.

He checked the cords on First Church's copier. Satisfied the machine had been properly plugged in, he lifted the cover and inspected the glass then opened the front drawer and checked the drum. As he suspected, the drum needed to be cleaned.

"Won't take long, Mrs. Reynolds. I just need to clean the drum," said Ben.

The middle-aged secretary with short salt-and-pepper hair rubbed her hands together. "That's wonderful, Ben. I still need to print the bulletins, and it's almost time to go home. If I don't have Ray's supper fixed by five, he whines like a starved puppy. Honestly, you'd think the man never ate a meal in his life, but I fix him breakfast and lunch, and then..."

Mrs. Reynolds rattled on about the many things her husband did and didn't expect from her. Ben grinned and nodded and continued to work. She was one of the sweetest members of the congregation and absolutely crazy about her cranky husband. But man, could that woman talk. Which, now that Ben thought about it, might be the reason Ray Reynolds was so cranky. The notion made Ben grin all the more.

The office bell rang, announcing that someone had arrived at the church. Ben would have a moment's reprieve while she talked with whoever came through the door.

"Hi, Mrs. Reynolds. Aunt Jane just wanted me to stop by and pick up the Sunday school material for her class."

Ben turned at Maggie's voice. She looked at him, a

blush blooming on her cheeks, then she glanced back at Mrs. Reynolds.

"Of course, dear."

The secretary took the materials out of a box beside Ben then started telling Maggie about dinner plans for that evening. Ben hurried to finish the drum. After putting his equipment back in the briefcase, he closed the front of the copier. "All done, Mrs. Reynolds."

Both women looked at him. Mrs. Reynolds placed the original bulletin in the tray and started the copies. She clapped. "Hooray. Thanks so much, Ben."

Embarrassment wrapped around him when she turned to Maggie and patted him on the back. "Such a good boy. I'm sure you've gotten to work with Ben at the Jacobs's farm. Isn't he just the hardest worker? Just like the rest of the family."

Maggie averted her gaze. "Yes, well. I've got to be going."

Ben shook Mrs. Reynolds's hand. "Me, too. I'll see you Sunday."

He started to walk out, but she grabbed his arm. "But what about a bill? How much does the church owe you?"

Ben watched Maggie as she walked out of the building. He had to hurry before she got away. "It's covered, Mrs. Reynolds, with the church's insurance."

"Oh, well, terrific. That's…"

The phone rang, and Ben lifted a quick prayer of thanks as she picked up the phone and he waved goodbye. Maggie was in her car by the time he got outside. His boots crunched against the snow-covered parking lot. He waved to her, and she hesitantly rolled down the window.

"Hi, Maggie."

She looked past him, beside him. Everywhere but at him. "Hi."

"I didn't get to thank you for dinner the other night."

Though he wanted to spend real time with her, he couldn't help but inwardly chuckle at the memory. She dropped silverware, dripped food on her lap and spilled Pete's drink in her effort to avoid him. Before he could thank her, she'd begged a headache and gone to her room to lie down.

She stuck the key in the ignition. "It was no big deal. Thanks for clearing the sidewalk and parking lot."

"Maggie, I'd like to…"

"I've got to go, Ben. It was nice talking to you." She turned the ignition, but the car didn't start. It didn't even make a noise.

"Is something wrong?"

"I'm sure it's nothing." She took the key out of the ignition then put it back in. Still nothing from the car.

"Pop the hood. Let me have a look."

Maggie blew out a long breath, and he knew it pained her to have him look at the car. He also knew she didn't have any other choice. He checked the hoses and fuses. Everything looked to be in good shape. He glanced around the hood. "Let me try to jump it. Hang on."

After pulling the work truck next to hers and attaching the jumper cables, he told her to turn the ignition. The car still didn't start.

"Everything okay out here?" Mrs. Reynolds stood just outside the door, her hands wrapped around her arms.

Ben waved. "Yes. I'm going to take Maggie home. Thanks, though."

Maggie hopped out of the car and slammed the door. She rubbed her eyes and forehead with both hands. "What do you think is wrong with it?"

"Pretty sure it's the starter."

Maggie groaned. "I wonder how much that will cost."

"I'm going to fix it."

Maggie looked up at him. It was the first time in weeks they'd locked gazes, and Ben relished the cool blueness of her eyes. They reminded him of the sky on a clear summer day. "Ben." She broke the gaze.

"I mean it, Maggie." He nodded to the truck. "I'm taking you home first."

She opened her mouth to argue then shut it just as fast. After grabbing several things from the car, she got in his truck. He shut the hood of the car and put the jumper cables in the back of the truck then hopped in the cab beside her.

She stared straight ahead. "Why are you doing this, Ben?"

"Because I care about you." *Because I love you.* The words clung to the tip of his lips. He would say them, as soon as he'd proven she could trust him.

Chapter 19

The lights went out.

"Mommy, the TV quit woking," Pete called from the living room.

"Hang on, honey," Maggie called back.

"My sewing machine stopped, too," said Aunt Jane from her craft room.

"I'm checking the breaker." Maggie opened the breaker box in the laundry room. She flipped each switch, but the electricity did not come back on. "Oh, no."

She placed her hand against her mouth, raced back into the kitchen, then looked at the bill on the counter. The cutoff for the electricity was today.

She turned to her aunt, who now stood beside her. Embarrassment flooded her. "It's the electric bill. I couldn't pay it."

Aunt Jane's expression softened and pity marked her features. "Maggie, it's time to…"

The front door opened, and her mom's voice rang through the room. "I'm here. I made it."

Tears swelled in Maggie's eyes. How could she have forgotten? She'd written it on the calendar and reminded herself before bed last night. The plan had been to run to town right after breakfast. Then Pete spilled his bowl of cereal, and she'd gotten distracted cleaning the mess and changing his clothes before her mother showed up for a visit. "I'm so sorry, Aunt Jane."

Without greeting her mom, she rushed past her aunt to the bedroom and shut the door. Hot tears trailed down her cheeks, and she pressed her face into the pillow. She'd failed. Despite the effort, the hard work, she couldn't keep the property afloat.

The bedroom door opened, and her mom walked in. "Hey, Maggie. Why don't you go with me to get the electricity turned back on?"

Maggie couldn't look at her mom. "Mom, I..."

"You've done everything you can to keep this place going. Aunt Jane tells me every week about your hard work. You have no reason to be embarrassed."

Hearing the words aloud, Maggie choked back a sob. She just didn't understand why the funds wouldn't come together. She'd prayed. Hard. Been faithful. Laid the bills at the foot of the cross, just as she'd been taught.

God had brought her to Bloom Hollow to help her aunt. She'd been so sure the move was God's guidance. Even her pastor and friends agreed the move would be good for her and Pete. So why couldn't she get their finances in good order? And why was God so quiet?

Her mom wrapped her arm around Maggie. "Come with me. We'll stop and get burgers for dinner on the way home."

Humiliated, she followed her mother to the car. She

couldn't get out when her mom went inside the electric company and paid the bill. On the way back to the house they stopped to buy fast food and then headed home. "Aunt Jane and I have talked about it. We're selling the property."

Maggie stared through the windshield. "I know."

"She's going to go back with me when I leave."

Maggie turned to her mom. "What?"

"That's why I came." She placed her hand on Maggie's arm. "She wants to move."

"Because I failed."

"No. Because it's time."

Maggie didn't respond. What could she say? Nothing. She had no defense. No way to make things happen. They pulled into the driveway, and Maggie motioned to her own car. "I need some time alone. Do you mind…"

Mom leaned over and kissed her forehead. "I understand. Take some time. Pray about this. Moving is the right thing."

Numb to her core, Maggie drove. She had nowhere to go. She wanted to talk to Tammie or Callie or Pamela. Or Ben. Or go to the farm, where she could walk through the orchard or swing on the swings. The frigid temperature wouldn't faze her at this moment.

She found herself parked in front of the church. No one was there. Figuring the door was locked, she went up the steps and tried the door, anyway. Locked, just as she expected.

She sat back in the driver's seat of the car. Resting her head against the steering wheel, she closed her eyes. "God, I was so sure you wanted me to come to Bloom Hollow. To help Aunt Jane. To start fresh."

She thought of Paul. How much she loved him. How excited he'd been when she told him they were expecting.

Finances hadn't been easy. They lived on his income. But they'd been in the midst of God's will, and they'd been happy. Then Paul died.

"God, I've come to grips with Paul's death. I miss him, but I'm so thankful to have part of him here in Pete. When Aunt Jane mentioned she might sell the family's house and shop, I was just sure you wanted me here. But I've failed, God. Why would You want me here if You knew I would fail?"

Maggie leaned her head back against the headrest and stared at the ceiling of her car. "What am I going to do now, God? What do you want for Pete and me?"

As the words left her lips, she heard a car pull up beside her. She leaned forward and wiped her eyes then turned to look at who had come to the church. A man walked toward the passenger's side of the car then bent down and looked inside. Ben.

Ben bent down beside Maggie's car. He'd promised the Properties Committee chairman that he would check out the audio system due to a slight buzzing sound in certain microphones. He didn't expect anyone to be at the church, especially not Maggie.

He noted her red, puffy eyes, and the frown pulling down her beautiful lips. "Maggie, are you all right?"

Clamping his mouth shut, he inwardly berated himself for the foolish question. She was obviously upset, but what was she doing sitting outside the church?

To his surprise, she stepped out of the car and stared up at him. He couldn't move for the intensity in her gaze. "Maggie?"

In a flash, she covered the distance between them, wrapped her arms around his waist and pressed her face against his chest. Stunned, he accepted her embrace and held her close while she cried. His left arm held tight while he ran his right hand through her hair. "It's okay," he murmured, not knowing what else to say, but determined to do whatever it took to assure her he would protect her, help her, love her—whatever she needed. And all of the above.

She loosened her grip then wiped her eyes with her fingertips, smudging mascara all over her face. Ben wiped at the makeup.

"I'm a mess, aren't I?"

He grinned. "A beautiful mess."

She offered a half smile.

"Come on." He grabbed her hand. "I need to check on the audio system. You can go clean up in the bathroom, then we'll talk."

He unlocked the church, and Maggie headed straight for the bathroom while he checked on the equipment. After tightening a few wires and conducting a sound check, the audio system was ready. He looked around and noticed Maggie sitting in a pew to his left, dabbing her eyes with a tissue. He went down and sat beside her. "Maggie, what is it?"

"I've failed." Her lower lip quivered, and she wiped her eyes again.

"What do you mean?"

"We're selling the house and shop. I couldn't keep it open." She sniffed. "Aunt Jane has lived there her entire life. Now she has to move because of me."

Ben shook his head. "Your aunt has been talking about selling for a couple of years. She even told my mom that. I don't think you've failed…"

"She wouldn't have, though." Maggie's eyes, swollen and red, seemed to carry the weight of the world. "I was so sure God was telling me to move to Bloom Hollow to help her." She shrugged. "I just couldn't keep it going. She's packing." She waved her hand. "Maybe even right now. Mom is visiting, and she's going back with Mom."

Panic swelled in Ben's stomach. "What about you and Ben?"

"I don't know. Mom and Aunt Jane have been doing all the talking. I don't know if we'll stay to help sell it, or if they want us to go." Fresh tears flowed and she wiped them with the tissue. "I don't even know where I'm supposed to live."

He knew where she should live. With him. As his wife. "Maggie, you were supposed to move to Bloom Hollow, but what if it wasn't to save your aunt's property?"

She frowned and rubbed her temples with her fingertips.

"What if you and Pete moved here for me?" Ben knelt down beside her. He wished he'd brought the ring with him. But how would he have known he'd be proposing tonight? Trepidation washed over him and he shivered. *Oh, God, give me the right words to say.*

"What do you mean?" She shifted in the pew, and her eyes widened as she looked at him. "Ben, what are you doing?"

Ben grabbed her hand. "Maggie, I love you. With all my heart, I love you. And I love Pete. As if he were my own son. I believe God sent you here for me, Maggie. To be my wife."

Maggie pulled her hand back and jumped to her feet. "Ben, what are you saying?"

He sat back in the pew. His heart pounded in his chest. He opened his arms wide, his embarrassment shifting to frustration. He'd done everything he could think of to prove to Maggie that he was worthy of her love. That he'd take care of her and Pete. Keep them safe. Devote his life to them. "I think it's obvious what I'm saying. Maggie, I want to marry you."

Maggie gasped. She gripped a chunk of hair on each side and shook her head. "I've got to go." Then she ran out of the building.

Ben stared at the door as humiliation seeped into his pores. He'd made a complete fool of himself.

His cell phone buzzed, and he pulled it out of his pocket. Taylor's name flashed on the screen. He almost laughed out loud. Perfect timing. He hadn't felt this low in a long time, not even when he'd embarrassed himself in the interview back in January.

He shoved his phone back into his pocket and looked at the wooden cross at the front of the sanctuary. Gambling no longer had a hold on him. He wouldn't be foolish enough to go to a friend's house where a game was set up. And he no longer felt the urge to seek one out. Even if he was embarrassed. Hurt.

He loved Maggie to the depths of his core, but the time had come to let her go. He had to trust that God knew best. If that meant Maggie would move away— the thought sent a physical pain through his heart—then he'd have to let her go.

Maggie opened the front door. Her mom sat on the couch with Pete curled up next to her sound asleep. Mom lifted her finger to her lips, and Maggie couldn't help but grin despite the unbelievable events of the day.

As she lifted Pete into her arms, she spied two cardboard boxes filled with Aunt Jane's things on the floor beside the chair. She sucked in a deep breath and took Pete to the bedroom. Gently, she undressed him and put on his pajamas. Tucking him into bed, she kissed his forehead then made her way to the kitchen.

Aunt Jane's bedroom door was already shut. Maggie opened the refrigerator to find something to eat and saw a chicken salad.

"Yes, the chicken salad is for you," said her mom from the living room.

Maggie grinned. She must have heard the refrigerator door open. A mom never stopped being a mom, she supposed. "Thanks, Mom," Maggie called back.

Getting her food and drink together, Maggie headed back into the living room and curled up in the chair across from her mom.

"You okay?" asked Mom.

"Still feel like a failure."

"She's wanted to sell a long time, Maggie. She let you come here to try to keep the place going for *you,* not for her."

Maggie pointed the plastic fork at herself. "For me? No. You should see the sadness in Aunt Jane's eyes…"

"That sadness is for you."

Maggie paused and swallowed a bite of salad. "Why?"

"She wants you to be happy, Maggie. Paul's death was hard. She wanted you to have a fresh start."

Maggie blinked and allowed her mother's words to settle into her mind and heart. *Fresh start.* Those were her thoughts. Over and over again. *Help Aunt Jane. Get a fresh start.* She stared at Mom. "She really wanted to sell?"

"For years, Maggie." Mom curled her legs under her. "Didn't you notice at Christmas how much she enjoyed being at my house? She picked the colors for her bedroom. Told me what to buy. Even paid for it."

Maggie took another bite of salad. "When?"

"Before you moved here."

Maggie opened her mouth then shut it. That explained

why her aunt's bank account had been so low when Maggie moved in. She hadn't been planning to stay much longer. "But what about me and Pete? I left my apartment in Texas."

"You could always move in with me for a while."

Maggie glared at her mother.

Mom laughed. "I didn't think you'd want that, so Aunt Jane and I decided you could stay here until the place sells. I'll take over the payments, but you'll have to take care of utilities."

Maggie nodded. She could handle that arrangement. Taking another bite of salad, her thoughts drifted to Ben. The wounded expression on his face when she'd run out chipped away at her.

"Something else is bothering you," said Mom.

Maggie set the plastic bowl on the end table. Should she tell Mom about Ben? Talking about him might be painful, and yet Maggie needed advice. Desperately.

"Is it about that boy?"

Maggie hadn't told her mom about anyone.

"Aunt Jane said his name is Ben."

Maggie gasped. "Aunt Jane told you about Ben?"

"She did." Her mom clasped her hands in her lap. "I'd be willing to bet she told me everything about Ben."

Maggie leaned back in the chair and pushed the footrest out. "Not everything."

"You mean his gambling?"

"No, I mean his proposing."

Mom's eyes widened. "He proposed?"

Maggie narrowed her gaze. "You know he gambles."

Mom lifted her finger. "Gambled. According to Aunt Jane. And there is a big difference."

Maggie picked at the piece of raveling fabric on the afghan on the arm of the chair. "He says he doesn't gamble now, but I'm afraid, Mom. I don't want to go through what you did, and I don't want Pete to go through it."

"Aunt Jane tells me he's been shoveling the sidewalk, clearing the parking lot, changing the starter in your car at no cost to you. Do you remember your dad doing any of those things?"

Maggie shook her head. "Not while he was gambling."

"And she says he's a Christian. That he's made a commitment to God and his family."

Maggie nodded.

"Your dad never did any of those things."

Maggie stared at the afghan. She traced the outline of the flower and leaves. "I know."

"Do you love him?"

Maggie closed her eyes and nodded again. "But I'm scared. What if he gambles again?"

"There are no promises in life. You'll have to decide if you're willing to take that chance."

Maggie breathed in and out, begging God to give her some kind of sign. Some kind of assurance that Ben would never hurt her. Then she realized He wouldn't. God had given Ben free will to choose to gamble or to follow Him. In her heart, Maggie knew Ben followed God, but she had been going her own way, not really trusting Him with her life, her money, or with love. *Forgive me, Lord.* Peace filled her spirit, and she knew she would step out in faith.

"So, when did he propose?" asked her mom.

"Tonight."

Mom chuckled. "What?"

"Yeah. I left here, drove to the church to pray and Ben showed up." She remembered her words to God, asking him what He wanted for her and Pete. Then Ben was there. *God, I've been so blind.*

"How would he know you were there?"

"He didn't. He went to fix the audio system."

"And he asked you."

Maggie nodded.

"What did you say?"

"I stood up and ran out."

Her mom opened her mouth and formed an "O" with her lips.

Maggie smiled. "But now I think I know what my answer is going to be."

Chapter 20

Ben knocked on the front door. Aunt Jane opened it and motioned for him to come inside. "Pete's been looking forward to you coming all day."

"I was a little surprised you called." He looked around the room stacked with boxes. His gut churned at the thought that Maggie and Pete would soon be moving away from him.

An older version of Maggie walked into the room, and Ben remembered his mother telling him and Kirk if they wanted to know what their wives would look like as they got older, to look at their mothers. Well, Maggie's mother was beautiful. He extended his hand. "You must be Maggie's mother."

"Call me Sandy. And you must be Ben."

"I am."

Pete ran into the room, already wearing his coat and hat. "I'm ready to go, Mr. Ben."

Ben took Pete's hand and waved to Sandy. "It was nice meeting you."

"I hope to meet again soon."

Ben buckled Pete into his booster seat. "Does your mom know you're playing with me and the boys today?"

Pete shrugged. "I dunno. Mommy's been gone all day."

Ben drove to the house and barely made it to the end of the driveway before Pete tried to bust out of his seat and race into Kirk and Callie's house. Kirk opened the door. "Get in here. The game's about to start."

"What about the boys?"

"Emma and Emmy are here. They'll help with the boys."

"Where's Pamela?"

Jack pulled a bag of popcorn out of the microwave and dumped it in a bowl. "She didn't say. Just said she was leaving."

"She left with Callie," said Kirk.

"And your mom," added Dad.

Ben chuckled. "You let the women go on a girl date during a March Madness basketball game when UT is playing Kentucky?"

Jack motioned toward the hall. "You have a kid here, too, you know."

He felt as if a fist grabbed his heart and twisted it. He wished Pete was his son, but Maggie had made herself pretty clear two nights ago. She'd probably be furious when she discovered Jane had asked him to watch Pete while she and Maggie's mom finished packing.

"Where's the chips and salsa?" asked Dad.

Kirk growled. "Dad, you were supposed to bring the salsa."

Dad pulled a jar out of a grocery bag. "Just kidding."

They grabbed soft drinks out of the fridge then carried their snacks to the living room. Ben checked on the kids and was pleased to see Emma and Emmy had everything well under control.

He settled onto the couch, and took a drink of his Coke.

Kirk lifted up the remote control. "The beauty of modern technology. If we have any child calamities, we can pause the game, tend to the trauma, then start her back up."

"What about lunch?" asked Ben.

"You didn't see the boxes of pizza in the kitchen?" asked Jack.

"Or smell them?" added Dad.

Ben lifted his hands in surrender. "Sorry. Just checking."

The truth was Ben had been missing a lot the past two days. Waking up late. Dropping and having to refix things at work. He hadn't told anyone about his impromptu proposal, but her response haunted him. She hadn't said no. If she'd just said no, he might have handled the rejection better. Or maybe not.

But for her to jump up, grab her hair and run out of the church as if the building was on fire—he'd never expected that. He couldn't decide if she was repulsed, angry or confused. Whatever she was, her response wasn't a positive one, and he wished he could take back his words.

The game started, and Kentucky won the tip-off. His dad cheered for Tennessee's guard to block the shooter. Kentucky's guard shot and missed. The guys cheered, and Kirk spilled some of his popcorn. He didn't seem to mind, simply ate the fallen pieces first then dug back into the bowl.

Pete tugged on Ben's shirtsleeve. "Whatcha doin'?"

"Watching a basketball game." He patted the seat beside him. "You wanna watch it with me?"

Pete nodded, and Ben lifted him onto the couch. Pete grabbed a pretzel from Ben's bowl and snuggled up beside him. The game continued, and Pete never left Ben's side. He cheered when Ben did and booed when Ben did.

At halftime, they got the kids together and fed them pizza. Emma and Emmy cleaned up the kitchen while Kirk put the twins down for a nap. Pete never left Ben's side.

When the game came back on, Pete nestled into the crook of Ben's arm. Before the third quarter ended, he'd fallen asleep. Ben cuddled him closer, determined to relish every moment of this afternoon. He might never see Pete again, or if he did, the meeting might be in passing.

He wanted to be a father to the boy. To teach him to ride a horse and throw and catch a ball. He loved the little guy.

The game ended. Tennessee lost. The whole state was even having a disappointing day. He called Jane's number to see when she wanted him to take Pete back to the house.

"We're not ready quite yet. Is it all right if I call you? He's not any trouble, is he?" she asked.

Ben nestled the sleeping child closer. "He's no trouble at all. I just didn't want you...or Maggie...to be worried."

"No worry at all, Ben. Thanks so much for the help."

She clicked off the phone, and Ben put his cell phone on the end table.

"Guess I'll be here a little while longer." He pointed to Pete. "Least until he wakes up."

Kirk shrugged. "No problem. He and the boys can play after their naps."

"Okay. Thanks." Ben placed his elbow on the arm of

the chair then rested his cheek on his fist. He stared at the screen, watching Kentucky's fans bask in their victory.

"You seem a little bummed," said Jack.

Kirk pointed to the TV. "Tennessee just lost, man."

Ben grinned at his brother.

Jack rolled his eyes. "It's probably a little more than that. Wanna talk about it?"

Ben shook his head. *It* was the last thing he wanted to talk about.

"I can't believe it's the middle of March, and you just now used the spa certificate Ben got you for Christmas," said Pamela.

"I would have used it the first week," said Tammie. She giggled as she cupped her mouth with her hand. "I mean, I did."

Callie lifted her brows. "And you didn't mind coming back again, did you, Tammie?"

Tammie shook her head. "Not at all." She touched Maggie's hand. "Anytime you want an all-girl spa day, you give me a call."

Maggie relaxed against the padded leather chair as a young dark-haired woman filed her toenails. She'd never had a facial or a massage before today. Her skin tingled, and her muscles ached with pleasure and contentment. "I think I'm hooked," she mumbled.

"I hear ya," said Callie. "After a long week with the boys fighting colds, this is just what I needed."

Maggie leaned forward to see all three of them. "I do have a reason for asking you all to come here with me today."

"I bet I know," said Pamela. "Ben proposed."

Maggie's jaw dropped. "How would you know that?"

"I was just kidding." Pamela's foot fell into the spa

water, splashing the technician in the face. The woman glared at her, and Pamela grabbed a towel off the side of the chair and tried to wipe the lady's face. The woman took the towel and pointed at the foot rest. Pamela cringed. "I'm so sorry." She looked at Maggie. "That was a joke. Ben really asked you to marry him?"

Maggie looked at Tammie, who shook her head with her hand covering her mouth. Tears glistened in her eyes. "Oh, Maggie, Maggie, Maggie."

"That is wonderful." Callie fanned her eyes with her hands. "I can't believe little Benny is getting married."

Maggie wrinkled her nose. "Well, it's not quite that simple."

"You said no?" said Callie.

Pamela's face dropped, and she glared at Maggie.

"Ben loves you," said Tammie. "It's so obvious. I know you're nervous about his past, but…"

"Girl, I can tell you a thing or two about getting past somebody's past," said Pamela.

Callie nodded. "Ben's changed, Maggie. He hasn't gambled in almost a year. He's dedicated to the Lord, and I can see how much he cares about you and Pete, and…"

"I thought you loved him, too," said Tammie. "I see it in your eyes when you're with him, Maggie, dear. You just need to open your heart."

Maggie lifted both hands in the air and accidentally pulled her foot back. The technician painted her entire toe then looked up at Maggie and shook her head. Maggie dipped her chin. "I'm sorry." She looked back at Tammie, Callie and Pamela. "You are all correct."

The three smiled, and Pamela said, "So you told him yes."

"No, I didn't."

Maggie shared about the electricity being turned off,

her mom arriving at the house and driving to the church to pray. She told them how he proposed, her response, her confusion and her talk with her mom. By the time she'd finished, Maggie blew out a long breath and leaned back against the chair again. The past few days had been just as exhausting as the past four years.

Callie frowned. "So I don't get it. What do you want us to do?"

Maggie grinned. "I want you to help me come up with a fun way to tell Ben that I want to marry him. And I want to tell him tonight."

Pamela rubbed her hands together and straightened her shoulders. Her technician tapped her leg then lifted her pointer finger and waved it back and forth so that Pamela wouldn't move.

Tammie chuckled and swatted her daughter's arm. "Would you sit still for that poor woman?"

"Well, what do you have in mind? A romantic dinner?" asked Callie.

"Actually, Mom and Aunt Jane are packing her things. She's going back with Mom tomorrow. I'll stay in the house until it sells."

"Or until you get married," said Pamela.

Excitement rushed down Maggie's spine at that thought. "Yes. So Aunt Jane asked Ben to watch Pete."

"Ben has Pete?" asked Callie.

"Mmm-hmm."

Callie cackled. "That means the guys had all the kids for the UT versus UK game today. I bet they were thrilled."

"Anyway," said Tammie. "Go on."

"I wanted to come up with a way that I could tell him in front of all of you." She swallowed back emotion. "I feel like you're my family, and I'll be marrying all of you, as well."

Callie nodded. "Trust me. You will."

Pamela crossed her arms in front of her chest. "You say that like it's a bad thing."

Callie shook her head. "Never." When Pamela and Tammie looked away, she mouthed, "Well, sometimes."

Maggie laughed, and Pamela and Tammie looked back at Callie. She lifted her hands. "What? I didn't say a word."

Pamela rolled her eyes then intertwined her fingers with her pointer fingers raised up and tapping back and forth. "Hmm."

Tammie leaned forward. "I think I have an idea."

Ben nearly jumped out of his skin when Callie ran into the house. She didn't say a word, just marched around the house wearing the silliest smile he'd ever seen.

"Is something the matter, Callie?" asked Kirk.

She stood up straighter. "Yes." She motioned toward the coatrack and then pointed to the door.

Kirk scratched his head. "You want me to go with you?"

"Yes." She pointed to Ben, Dad, Jack and all the kids.

"You want all of us to go?" asked Ben.

"Yes."

Dad stood up and placed the back of his hand against Callie's forehead. "Are you sick? Did you hit your head?"

Callie wrinkled her nose and swatted his hand away.

Kirk released an exaggerated sigh. "Really? We all have to go with you?"

"Yes."

"And you're only going to say yes?"

"Yes."

Ben chuckled as he slipped on his boots then put Pete's on, as well. Callie and Kirk got the boys ready while everyone put on their coats.

Dad said, "Okay. Where we going?"

Callie pointed to the B and B. "Yes."

Ben spied the car that had been in Maggie's driveway earlier that day. Her mom's car, he assumed. He exhaled a bit of disappointment. Jane must have told Sandy about the farm and she'd wanted to see it before they left. He'd hoped to run into Maggie when he took Pete back later in the day. Today might be his last chance to see her.

The twins and Pete raced to the house, with Callie and Kirk following behind. Ben couldn't make himself go any faster. Each step he took felt like he was drawing closer to the end of his time with Maggie and Pete. His heart broke at the thought.

Pamela stood in the yard blocking their way to the back door. She smiled at all of them but didn't say a word.

Dad motioned to the door. "Pamela, you gonna let us go in the house?"

She smiled. "Yes."

Ben shoved his hands into his pockets and looked at his brother-in-law. Jack moved toward her and kissed her cheek. "Are you going to let us in the house now?"

"Yes."

She moved out of the way, and they walked into the kitchen. Post-it notes covered the cabinets, the refrigerator, the stove. Everywhere. All of them had one word written in all caps. *YES.*

Ben looked at his mother, who stood in front of the door that led to the living room. "Mom, what are you all doing?"

"Yes," she answered. She blinked multiple times then

shifted her hip to cover the open space when Ronald tried to slip past her and into the living room.

Callie scooped the boy into her arms, then Pamela picked up Ronald.

Dad scratched his jaw. "Tammie Jacobs, is there a reason you girls are acting so silly?"

"Yes."

Kirk opened his hands. "Are you going to tell us what the reason is?"

"Yes."

"Is anyone going to say anything besides 'yes'?" boomed Dad.

Mom, Callie and Pamela exchanged glances then shrugged.

Mom grabbed Ben by the front of his shirt then pushed him into the living room first. He glanced back at his mom and scowled.

"Whatcha doin', Mommy?"

At Pete's question, Ben turned and saw Maggie standing on the other side of the living room. Just like the kitchen, Post-it notes covered the walls, the TV, the bookshelf. Looking around, he saw that Sandy and Jane sat in two of the chairs. The family walked in, and Dad asked, "What's going on?"

Maggie cleared her throat but she never took her eyes off Ben. He was trapped in her gaze, and he never wanted to be loosened. "Ben, you asked me a question two nights ago, and I never really gave you an answer."

Ben's heartbeat raced and his chest tightened.

"If you've been listening or looking around, you'll know what my answer is."

Ben covered the distance between them, picked her up off the floor and twirled her around.

"What was the question?" asked Dad.

"What's she talking about?" said Jack.

"We'll tell you later," said Mom.

Ben kissed her forehead then grabbed her hand in his. "Come with me real quick."

She nodded, and he guided her through the sea of family. Some with confused expressions. Some with tears glistening in their eyes. He guided her to the cabin, threw open the door and pointed to the living area. "Wait here."

He rushed into his bedroom and took the engagement ring out of the box. He put it in his jeans pocket then walked back to the living room. "Let's do this right."

Kneeling on one knee, he took the ring out of his pocket and held it up. "Maggie Grant, I am absolutely crazy in love with you. Will you marry me?"

Maggie nodded and said, "Yes."

He stood and wrapped his arms around her. She tilted her head back, and he lowered his lips to hers. He feared his heart would explode with thanksgiving as he devoured the sweet promise of forever in their kiss. He lifted his head. "I thought you'd never speak to me again."

"I was afraid."

"I know. I had to cling to the hope…"

"That I would find the faith to trust you to God?"

"Yes." With his thumb, he lifted her chin again. Her lips tasted just as sweet the second time. "My hope was found."

She kissed him once more. "And mine."

Chapter 21

"Are you ready?" asked Maggie's mom, Sandy.

"So ready," said Maggie.

Her mom beamed. "You look beautiful."

Maggie looked down at the simple full-length ivory satin gown. Thin straps draped her shoulders allowing the front to dip into a V. A thin satin sash wrapped around her waist and tied in a bow in the back. No beading. No lace. A simple satin dress, and she felt amazingly beautiful and elegant. Deciding against a veil, she turned her head so her mom could see her hair in the back. "Is the comb still in place?"

"The roses and baby's breath still look lovely. You're the picture of elegance."

Maggie grinned at her mom. "You have to say that."

Her mom kissed her cheek. "No, I have the privilege to say it."

The music started and the doors of the church opened.

Maggie saw her sister, Pamela, Callie, Emma and Emmy standing to the left of the altar. They looked beautiful in their simple pink dresses with wide green sashes around their waists. Kirk, Jack and one of Ben's friends from work stood to the right. She almost chuckled aloud at the silly grins on their faces.

Mike and Tammie sat on the front pew with Ronald and Teddy. Aunt Jane sat beside them, and Maggie smiled as her aunt pointed toward her and Ronald clapped his hands.

Her mom squeezed her arm, and they took their first step forward. A camera flashed several times, and Maggie blinked away the light spots. Her gaze locked on Ben. In a matter of moments, he would be her husband. She would be his wife.

Pete stood in front of him, his shoulders back and his chin up. He'd insisted he and Ben match, as he mimicked everything Ben said or did. Emotion swelled within her. Her men. How she loved them.

When she and her mom got close enough, Maggie saw Ben's bottom lip quiver, and he brushed a tear from his eye. As if on cue, Pete wiped a fake tear from his eye, as well. Paul would approve of Ben. He'd be happy that Pete had such a wonderful man to model his life after. A knot formed in her throat at the truth of the thought. Swallowing it back, she silently praised God for what had to be the millionth time for allowing her to find true love a second time.

The minister called for her to join hands with Ben. She stared into his eyes, relishing the sincerity and love radiating from them. His promise of honor, loyalty, respect, protection—he meant the words to the core of his being, and she could feel the promise in her heart.

With the I dos said and the announcement of marriage made, Ben cupped her cheeks with his hands. "I love you, Maggie Jacobs."

Hearing her new name on his lips sent a thrill of excitement through her. "I love you, too, Ben Jacobs."

He lowered his head and kissed her lips with urgency and anticipation. When he released her, she exhaled a sigh of pleasure. God had given her love once more.

* * * * *

REQUEST YOUR FREE BOOKS!

2 FREE INSPIRATIONAL NOVELS
PLUS 2
FREE
MYSTERY GIFTS

Love Inspired

Name _____ (PLEASE PRINT) _____

Address _____ Apt. #

City _____ State/Prov. _____ Zip/Postal Code

Signature (if under 18, a parent or guardian must sign)

REQUEST YOUR FREE BOOKS!

2 FREE INSPIRATIONAL NOVELS
PLUS 2
FREE
MYSTERY GIFTS

Love Inspired.

HISTORICAL
INSPIRATIONAL HISTORICAL ROMANCE

YES! Please send me 2 FREE Love Inspired® Historical novels and my 2 FREE mystery gifts (gifts are worth about $10). After receiving them, if I don't wish to receive any more books, I can return the shipping statement marked "cancel." If I don't cancel, I will receive 4 brand-new novels every month and be billed just $4.74 per book in the U.S. or $5.24 per book in Canada. That's a savings of at least 21% off the cover price. It's quite a bargain! Shipping and handling is just 50¢ per book in the U.S. and 75¢ per book in Canada.* I understand that accepting the 2 free books and gifts places me under no obligation to buy anything. I can always return a shipment and cancel at any time. Even if I never buy another book, the two free books and gifts are mine to keep forever.

102/302 IDN F5CY

Name	(PLEASE PRINT)	
Address		Apt. #
City	State/Prov.	Zip/Postal Code

Signature (if under 18, a parent or guardian must sign)

Mail to the Harlequin® Reader Service:
IN U.S.A.: P.O. Box 1867, Buffalo, NY 14240-1867
IN CANADA: P.O. Box 609, Fort Erie, Ontario L2A 5X3

Want to try two free books from another series?
Call 1-800-873-8635 or visit www.ReaderService.com.

* Terms and prices subject to change without notice. Prices do not include applicable taxes. Sales tax applicable in N.Y. Canadian residents will be charged applicable taxes. Offer not valid in Quebec. This offer is limited to one order per household. Not valid for current subscribers to Love Inspired Historical books. All orders subject to credit approval. Credit or debit balances in a customer's account(s) may be offset by any other outstanding balance owed by or to the customer. Please allow 4 to 6 weeks for delivery. Offer available while quantities last.

Your Privacy—The Harlequin® Reader Service is committed to protecting your privacy. Our Privacy Policy is available online at www.ReaderService.com or upon request from the Harlequin Reader Service.

We make a portion of our mailing list available to reputable third parties that offer products we believe may interest you. If you prefer that we not exchange your name with third parties, or if you wish to clarify or modify your communication preferences, please visit us at www.ReaderService.com/consumerschoice or write to us at Harlequin Reader Service Preference Service, P.O. Box 9062, Buffalo, NY 14269. Include your complete name and address.

LIHDIR13R

ReaderService.com

Manage your account online!

- Review your order history
- Manage your payments
- Update your address

*We've designed
the Harlequin® Reader Service
website just for you.*

Enjoy all the features!

- Reader excerpts from any series
- Respond to mailings and
  special monthly offers
- Discover new series available to you
- Browse the Bonus Bucks catalog
- Share your feedback

Visit us at:
ReaderService.com

RS13